On Miriam Kotzin's *Country Music*

The 26 stories in *Country Music* read 20th midcentury history through as many lenses as a bee's eye. The title story would do Willy Nelson proud though my favorite is "Red Tiger," whose golden eyes hunt/ haunt us all. What a fabulous collection—it should become required reading in every American Studies program! *Country Music* is enormously entertaining, an impressive offering of fiction.

L. Shapley Bassen, author of *Summer of the Long Knives Lives*

What an engaging mixture of distinctive atmosphere, fluid prose, social insight (without condescension), and characterization the wonderful stories of *Country Music* are. I set aside an hour at work to read one or two and wound up taking the day off to read them all! We hear the evocative sound of Miriam Kotzin, gifted poet, in lines like this from the title story: "We got through mud-time just fine, and all through the spring we watched the little leaves unfold and the blue wash back into the sky." Or how about this sample of insight into human nature from "Devotional": "I have listened to Desirée as her marriage fell to pieces, and her revenge for having received my sympathy continues to play itself out in this small room." The stories of *Country Music* contain a set of perfectly written voices as original as I have ever listened to in fiction: this collection is absolutely recommended reading!

Lee Slonimsky, author of *Bermuda Gold*,
co-author (with Carol Goodman) of the *Black Swan Rising* trilogy

Miriam Kotzin is a prodigiously gifted writer (as her latest collection of stories *Country Music* amply demonstrates) whose work resonates in a remarkable number of genres—novels, poetry, stories, criticism, flash fiction, etc. In *Country Music* all her gifts, from her darkly hilarious satire to the way she can simply and lastingly touch our heart, are there for us to once again cherish. Miriam Kotzin is indisputably one of are country's most important women of letters.

Richard Burgin, editor of Boulevard, author of *Don't Think*

In *Country Music*, Miriam Kotzin presents a whole world: Driving lessons, young love, prom night, the Vietnam war; a boy who pees under a teacher's desk, a man who shoots mistletoe down from the oak trees; quiet battles over garden flamingoes and wedding cake; rape and domination; broken cups and broken marriages. The women are complex and wise, but hemmed in by strong events, and the men they love are complex and flawed. The women want the ideal world at the same time that they know the world is fallen. With its precise language, engaging characters, humor, and suspenseful action, *Country Music* is particularly notable for its heart and truth. Love in such a world is essential but almost impossible, and all the more worth aspiring to.

Cezarija Abartis, author of *Nice Girls and Other Stories*

The twenty-six stories in Miriam Kotzin's stellar collection, *Country Music*, range wide and deep in their deft and piercing exploration of emotion, relationships and characters in the crucibles of love, rivalry and strained friendships. The style is compressed and dynamic, narratives tightly structured and the language shaped to the narrator's origins, place and sensibility. Nothing is wasted, with characters portrayed—and occasionally betrayed—by every sentence thought or spoken, every choice made or avoided. She knows her people and after a while you know them too, and then the face looks awfully familiar indeed. In their individuality, again and again, these stories and their characters tap the vein of the universal.

David Ackley

Country Music

Miriam N. Kotzin

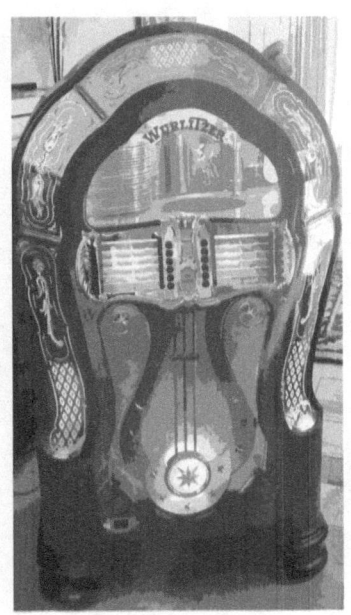

SPUYTEN DUYVIL
NEW YORK CITY

Acknowledgments

"At the Set Time," *Amarillo Bay*, November 2005; "Beauty Cannot Keep," *Offcourse*, fall, 2005; "Country Music," *Fiction Warehouse*, February 16, 2005; "Crush," *Southern Hum*, Winter, 2005-2006; "Devotional," *Absinthe Literary Review*, Eros and Thanatos, 2006; "Drowning," *Slow Trains*, June 2004; "Flamingos," *Delmarva Review* (November 2011), pp. 10-11; "Four Things I Found," *Suburban Fool*, January 31, 2012; "Hoops," *Amarillo Bay Literary Review* (May 2011); "Ice," *ELF: Eclectic Literary Forum*, Vol. 8, Number 2, Summer, 1998, pp. 6-9; "Liar," *Prime Number* 17.2 (February 2012); "Neighbor," *SaucyVox*, August, 2004; "No One Can Swim to the Moon," *Eclectica*, Fall 2005; "Secret," *Carve*, March 1, 2005; "Scar," *Cherry Bleeds*, November 2005; "Silver Queen," *Offcourse*, February 2007; "Sister," *Rose & Thorn*, December 2004; "Something to Celebrate," *Fiction Warehouse*, August 31, 2005; "Supervision," *Press 1* Vol. 5. 4 (Spring 2012). "Sugar Ants," *Flashquake* 11.2 (Spring 2012); "Surface Wounds," *Salome Magazine* December 5, 2011; "The Red Tiger," *Pindeldyboz*, January 11, 2006; "Upstream," *13th Warrior Review*, Vol. V. issue 9, Spring 2006; "Where You Want to Go," *Nuvein*, Fall 2005.

ISBN 978-1-944682-43-9

Library of Congress Cataloging-in-Publication Data

Names: Kotzin, Miriam N., 1943- author.
Title: Country music / Miriam N. Kotzin.
Description: New York : Spuyten Duyvil, [2017]
Identifiers: LCCN 2017001888 | ISBN 9781944682439
Classification: LCC PS3611.O74939 A6 2017 | DDC 813/.6--dc23
LC record available at https://lccn.loc.gov/2017001888

For Joe Danciger

Contents

COUNTRY MUSIC

Silver Queen

When she was far too young to understand, she overheard her momma talking about a mistake. Momma and Aunt Lou kept glancing over at her, but never once did either of them call her name until they'd drunk all the coffee, pouring from the bottle on the table.

Then it was: "Cora Mae, honey," Momma said, "take a dollar from the sugar bowl and run to the store to get Momma a pack of Luckies. Ask Uncle Bill to dip you an ice cream, any flavor you want. Then you come straight home, hear?" That's how long ago this happened.

"Aunt Lou," Cora Mae said, "you want somethin'?"

"No, Sugar," she said, "Just a big ole hug." She reached down and wrapped her arms around the girl.

Aunt Lou was soft as a marshmallow and smelled like sugar and jasmine and coffee and bourbon, she did, and each and every time she hugged her it felt like Aunt Lou was afraid it was the last, and she wanted to remember it for always and ever.

When Cora Mae had let the screen door slam, she hung back long enough to hear Momma ask, "What you gonna' do, Loulie?" And Cora Mae thought she'd go for the Luckies and ice cream after. She didn't know after what, just that there'd be something next, and she didn't want to miss it. Cora Mae'd only heard Momma call out "Loulie" once, when Aunt Lou's cat Sweetie-kitty had got herself treed, and Aunt Lou was crying like all get-out until Pete, who everyone said was sweet on her, came with a great big wood ladder and propped it up against a fat branch and got the cat down wrapped in a pink bath towel so it wouldn't scratch and handed Sweetie-kitty to Aunt Lou, who held her like a baby-doll.

And Pete, he told her she looked real pretty like that, and she'd make some man a good wife, and whoever he was he'd be right lucky to have her. And then Aunt Lou dropped the towel with the cat in it like she never cared a lick about Sweetie-kitty at all. And Sweetie-kitty was so surprised hitting the ground, she ran through the hole in the lattice work under the porch and stayed there all night. And Aunt Lou went into the house with the pink towel left in a heap on the lawn, and she didn't come out neither.

"What can I do?" she said. Her arms made a circle on the table, and she put her head down on her arms the way her first-graders did when they had their five-minute rest mid-morning while she played a '78 on her record player so they would have magic dreams though they weren't really expected to sleep at all. And when Aunt Lou lifted her head, Cora Mae couldn't see her face, and she was afraid to mash up against the screen and be caught listening. Cora Mae couldn't call her Aunt Lou in class and was supposed to call her Miz Taylor, and that never could come out of her mouth right, so she didn't call her by name at all. It didn't matter none. Everyone knew what they were to one another anyhow.

Momma scraped her chair back from the table and left the kitchen without saying a word. Cora Mae scrinched herself over to one side of the door, so if Momma glanced that way, she'd be more a shadow than anything. Of course, if Momma went to the door, she'd catch Cora Mae where she shouldn't be.

Momma was gone a long time, and all the while she was gone, Aunt Lou sat in that chair, her back as straight as Cora Mae had to sit on the piano bench when Miz Barlowe was teaching her posture. And Aunt Lou sat perfectly still though Cora Mae thought that maybe she could see her shoulders go up and down real slow. Sometimes she'd say to her class, "breathe in, breathe out, breathe," and she'd pause," breathe," another pause, "breathe." It was like breathing was something you had to think about and not something natural at all. And that's how she looked now, from the back, as though she was thinking about each breath.

Cora Mae knew it wasn't right to spy on kin, but she didn't mind doing some things that weren't right. She'd devil her Momma and devil her again by not seeming sorry for it. She wanted to rush in and give Aunt Lou a hug just as big and soft and sweet as the hugs Aunt Lou gave her, but if she did she wouldn't find out. It was something secret. Momma had that same sound in her voice she got with Poppa right after he got laid off.

She could run to the store and then run home if she had to. Run all the way. When Momma came back into the kitchen she had a square of white paper in her hand. She didn't say anything. She just put it on the table and pushed it over to where Aunt Lou was sitting.

Aunt Lou didn't pick it up. Not for a long time. Then Momma said, "You got to do something."

And Aunt Lou's shoulders they kept going up and down just as smooth and slow as you please, like she was still coaching herself on how to breathe. And Momma said, "Well, you got to, don't you?"

She waited a long time, but it was like her words went up in the air and got stuck on the strip of fly-paper hanging in a big curl over the table, and maybe Aunt Lou couldn't hear them because Momma's words were caught up there with all the big fat black houseflies. No matter how often Daddy cut down the paper and pulled a new curl free, there'd be flies. But if Cora Mae could hear, so could Aunt Lou so that wasn't why she didn't answer.

"You can't just go away this time. You know you can't." Momma sounded like she was in trouble and not Aunt Lou. Why was she so upset that Aunt Lou wouldn't take up the paper she'd brought? It wasn't that hard to carry a piece of paper from one room to the next, and Momma was acting like she'd brought in something heavy or a big chunk of gold and diamonds and Aunt Lou wasn't being proper grateful.

"Suppose...," Aunt Lou said. And then she didn't say anything else.

"What, Louise, suppose what?" Until right then Cora Mae had never heard her Momma say Louise. It was like she was talking to a person she didn't know, and, as much as she did know her, she didn't like her. Worse, she didn't mind none if she knew she didn't like her neither.

"You've got Cora Mae," Aunt Lou said real slow, her voice matching Momma's.

Then they sat like they were playing statues and Cora Mae had missed the start of the game where the rules got set out, but all of them knew whoever moved first would lose, and they were both waiting for the music to start to break the spell. They went a long time like that. Momma had a fan on the counter, and it turned to the left and to the right and picked up Momma's hair from her neck and then Aunt Lou's. It swept the table and the white square would lift up a bit and set right back down like it couldn't make up its mind whether to stay there or sail off where it couldn't cause no more trouble between them.

"You'll lose your job for sure."

"It's not supposed to happen like this," Aunt Lou said.

"What *were* you thinking?" Momma asked. And then she started to cry. "What'll happen to Cora Mae? How could you?"

What did this have to do with her?

"It wasn't supposed to," Aunt Lou said. She picked up the square of paper and folded it in fours, running her thumbnail down the creases to make them sharp and pushed the paper into her pocket. "I'll think about it."

"You have enough?" Momma asked.

Aunt Lou laughed like Momma told a joke on her, and she didn't like it. "What I need," she said, "what I need."

Cora Mae knew that she'd have to story if she didn't run to the store right then and get home with the Luckies.

And when she came home Momma and Aunt Lou were sitting across from one another at the picnic table with a newspaper spread out and piles of cornhusks and ears of sweet corn Aunt Lou had pulled that morning. And Cora Mae gave Momma the Luckies and the change, and neither woman thought to ask her about the ice cream or why she was out of breath. Aunt Lou patted the bench beside her for Cora Mae to sit down. And Aunt Lou showed her again the right way to husk corn and get off all the silk. It was good corn, with the rows all even and not squiggly. Silver Queen, she called it. Something new. And the summer went on, and then the fall and it all seemed just the way it had always been, and if you'd have asked the sisters they would have smiled and said, yes, thank you, they had what they needed, they had enough. And so they did.

COUNTRY MUSIC

The Cabin is one of those bars that has at least three pick-up trucks parked on the side no matter when, and inside it's dark and smells like beer as though a fine party had gone on the night before, and the place hasn't been aired out so there's a head start on the next good time. Just after my divorce, when Bill left with the television, I used to come here to watch "Jeopardy." I'd bring my daughter Rose Lee along, little as she was, and felt fine about it. Now I come here with my friends Mary Beth and Janice, I pay no mind to what's on the tube, and Rose Lee is just old enough to buy herself a legal drink.

The TV over the bar is always on, but unless it's a big game, nobody seems to look up at it. They might as well save the electricity. Weekend nights when there's likely to be dancing, the volume's turned down some, but even when somebody feeds the jukebox quarters the TV plays. In spite of the ladies' entrance, which no one ever uses, this is pretty much what the town has to offer in way of a night out.

Pete brought Jeff over to where we were sitting around a table and introduced us. Good looking. Freckles. Construction. Union. "I told Jeff that you ladies would make him feel right at home. Now don't go making a liar out of me."

Mary Beth kicked me under the table. So did Janice. Jesus. You'd think that no new men ever come to town. That we didn't know any first-rate men at all. All right, so if I'd been in a different mood, maybe I would have done a little kicking myself, or maybe even been willing to play a little footsie. But I'd just read another self-help book, and I'd given up on bad relationships, and I wasn't sure I was in the right mood for a good one.

Pete smiled. Jeff beamed. The three of us girls smiled right on back. My heart wasn't in it. I almost expected the draft from the fluttering eyelashes to blow the napkins off the table.

Or it might have been that last week was my old anniversary, reminding me how my ex-husband had come to town to do construction work on the new bank building where Rose Lee now works as a teller. We'd had a romance and got ourselves a head start on a family; no matter what else, I've never been sorry to have Rose Lee. Bill left fifteen years ago when she was seven, sent support checks regular until her twenty-first birthday, and doesn't live so far that they can't see each other.

But he stays far enough away from me so that now Rose Lee is grown he's no bother in my life at all. He's been a model ex-husband, and I don't regret his going. Past is past, but sometimes why I'd loved him so comes back to me like heat lightning in the evening sky.

Pete and Jeff went to get drinks for our table. Both of them were built sturdy. Pete's hair had gone gray early, and he had a bald spot that I used to like waking up to. In the last twenty years with the town small as it is, he'd spent a while with each of the three us, and though he wasn't one to kiss and tell details, at least not any more than we would, we supposed he would have said a few kind words about us to Jeff.

"What are we supposed to do, draw straws?" asked Janice.

"I don't think we'll have to do that," Mary Beth said, taking Janice at her word. "And when was the last time you saw a straw in a drink here?"

"I'll sit this one out," I said.

"Pauline." When they get on my case like this they kind of drag out the last part of my name so that it has three syllables. "What's wrong with you?"

"Nothing. I want to keep it that way."

"Well, he seems nice enough."

"He hasn't said five words. Jack the Ripper would seem nice

enough after just five words."

"Oh, give him a break."

"Give me one, will you."

When Pete and Jeff came back, we changed the topic and made small talk about Clayton. Jeff dropped crumbs of information about himself on the table as though he were feeding fish and waiting for them to rise to the surface to nibble.

Thirty-eight.

Divorced. Once.

One boy, eighteen, photo in wallet.

Can cook for himself.

Misses a woman's home cooking.

It was past midnight until I realized that Jeff was the kind of man I'd been warning Rose Lee about since she was old enough to say something about what underwear I put on when I had a date.

I was the first to leave. As I got up from the table, so did Jeff. He stood there, smiling at me, telling me with his eyes all the lies a woman wants to hear even when she knows better.

And that's how things began.

"What about your ex-husband?" he asked after our first night together. He stroked my hair at the temples, following the path where, if I took after my momma, in a few years the soft brown would sprout silver wings.

"Gone."

"That's it? Four letters. G-o-n-e?"

"Oh, there's more to him than that." No sense dragging my history out where it would clutter up the nice clean surface of our new relationship. He'd learn what he needed to as time went on. I suspected he was just poking to see whether what I told him jibed with what he'd heard from Pete. Men can be sneaky when they're figuring out what they want to do with a woman and for how long.

We got through mud-time just fine, and all through the

spring we watched the little leaves unfold and the blue wash back into the sky. We did the usual things—weekend nights at the Cabin or the movies, suppers and TV at home, and occasional weekend breakfasts at the Circle Diner, where Jeff liked the hotcakes and eggs with sausage. We talked about firing up his gas grill, but hadn't quite got around to it. What happened was fine, and what didn't happen didn't seem to matter. I wanted it to go on and on like that, easy, our time together a loose weave. Our love-making was always comfortable, and, sometimes, for me, being with him that way was like walking into a fancy hotel room and finding a fresh-made bed turned down to welcome me into it and with a gold-wrapped chocolate on the pillow, too.

My momma had always warned me that life gives you what you look for, so I tried not to look for trouble. I preferred having trouble sneak up behind me, tap me on the shoulder, tip his hat and say, "Pardon me, Ma'am..." So I thought everything was perfect until Janice and Mary Beth were shopping over in Bridgeton and told me they'd seen Jeff walking out of the Hilltop Tavern with Rose Lee's friend, Delia. And since he'd taken the trouble to go twenty miles for lunch and never mentioned it to me, I figured he had something to hide. From then on I watched to see how he acted with her, and I didn't much like what I saw. He stayed sweet as pie with me as long as I could pretend not to be noticing that sometimes he didn't call when he said he would and that after an early phone call he'd be out when I'd call him back.

For hours we'd been having a silent fight—you know the kind. Neither one of you admits something is wrong, because you know that what's wrong is something you don't want to acknowledge. It's like an animal has gone and died in the wall and the smell is there, and you think that if you pretend to ignore it, it will go away, but it doesn't, at least not for a long time. And what makes it bad is you know there's nothing you can do about it anyway. And even after you can only remember how it smelled, if you think about it at all, you know the little bones are walled up somewhere in your house.

I should have known not to argue with a man who'd just stepped in dog shit and tracked it over his kitchen floor before he smelled trouble.

He tossed his sneakers into the yard, probably smashing the geraniums I'd planted. Wearing his pathetic white socks, he used wads of paper towels to wash the mess up from the floor. He put the paper towels in the garbage. Then he filled the sink with detergent water and went out back with the garbage. He came in carrying his sneakers by their laces. He dangled them over the sink for a while before he lowered them real slow into the suds.

Up till then I had been pretty quiet. After the bad time we'd been having, I thought it would be better to hang back from this whole event. The sneakers disappeared into the sink where I'd fixed the salad for dinner and where I expected to get the water for morning coffee. I suppose I must've made some sound, because he wheeled around and snapped at me, "Did you say something?"

And then I said, "A bucket might be better."

We had a discussion on sanitary habits that had an awful lot to do with how I felt that he'd been paying too much attention to Delia and how he felt that I had no right to care about what he did with his time when he wasn't with me. But instead we said:

"They'll be easier to scrub in the sink."

"We use the sink for food."

"People put sneakers in the washer where they put sheets and towels. You can clean a sink easier."

"It's just not real appetizing, is it?"

"Clorox will disinfect the sink just fine."

"Do you have Clorox under there?" I knew he did. The kitchen and bathroom often stank of Clorox, which he used full strength.

"I'm just going to let them soak."

"What about the dishes?"

"They'll wait. Don't you ever do wash in the sink?"

"Are you comparing my underwear to dog shit?"

Sometimes I'm surprised how much tension a little infidelity can cause.

A few days later, I took a long lunch to try to make it up to him, and then I wished I hadn't been in the room when Delia called. I was sorry that I'd heard him talk to her, seen him brighten up like a polished teakettle so shiny I could see her face in it next to mine, with both our faces pushed out of shape for being there together.

When I answered the phone, I could have told her that she had the wrong number, but I was sure she'd just call back and he'd be mad at me. Besides, she knew who I was, and I didn't want her telling everyone that I'd tried to fool her. I suppose she didn't expect me to be at his place when I ought to have been working down at Clark's market.

So now Delia knew that he'd sweet-talk her right in front of me. That would make a good story that any one of the three of us could tell. It was a story I had sworn I would never be in again.

I hoped Delia wouldn't say anything to Rose Lee. I wanted to talk to her myself first. After the phone call and all through lunch, I'd sat staring at the pots of hot pink geraniums in the noon sun, hardly looking at Jeff at all. I tried. Over his shoulder the flowers pulled my attention away from his eyes, which I couldn't have seen anyway he was squinting so much. He almost never wears sunglasses, being vain about his hazel eyes and long lashes. Unless it's for one of those times when he can be dramatic and take off his aviators real slow; he wears them pushed up on his head where they take the light and bounce it around. For the rest of the summer, whenever I saw geraniums

I felt queasy.

These were the geraniums I'd brought to him and put in big white pots with ageratum to brighten up his yard a bit for times when I'd be here and especially for times when I wasn't. Male dogs piss on trees to mark territory and women plant flowers. For all the good it does.

I tried not to blame Rose Lee for this. Of course it wasn't her fault that Delia had pushed her way into my romance. I still like to say that she pushed her way in, but I know that's not what happened.

It's about two months now since Rose Lee told me about how Jeff had come over to the girls' booth at the Cabin, carrying his glass of beer. He smiled one of his wonderful smiles and plonked himself down next to Rose Lee, who pretty much on instinct slid over and made room for him. For the rest of the evening he'd turned the charm on both of them. Rose Lee, who should have heard enough about men, my men, to make her wary, came home with the story happy as though she was bringing me homemade jam.

She'd introduced him to Delia as my boyfriend, and after that, she took all that happened as pure friendliness. I might try to take some comfort that she's still so innocent. I knew there was trouble when she said, "I'm sorry for what I've been saying about him, Mom. I can see why you like him so much."

"Well, can you now," I said. "I'm real glad to hear that." I tried not to be too sarcastic.

For all the times Rose Lee and Jeff have been thrown together he'd never done much to charm her, so I knew right then that the high beams had been for Delia.

Jeff is only a couple of years younger than me, nothing to raise an eyebrow, even in this town, and Delia, who's got five years on Rose Lee, has never put up age limits on her beaux. When Rose Lee started hanging with her, I was worried, until I reminded myself that Rose Lee had never gotten into trouble while she was coming up, and with me as her mother at that. I kept my mouth shut, hoping they'd drift apart, but working together in the bank they stayed tight.

For the last couple of weeks Rose Lee hasn't talked much about Delia, and she's done a tap dance rather than answer any questions about her. And as for me, I guess I've been ignoring one of my major rules: never ask a question I don't want the answer to. Without knowing it Rose Lee was giving me the answers to all my questions, and I was kind of sorry I'd been asking.

I kept having a dream of seeing Jeff with Rose Lee and Delia. Jeff had his arm draped over each one, their arms wrapped around his waist, reached down and into his back pants pockets. I could feel them bumping together as they walked down the street with me caught behind them with no way to pass. The ground had opened up behind me so I couldn't turn my back on them and walk away.

I took to making a record of all the times things didn't match up—what Jeff said, what I heard, and what I didn't hear from Rose Lee. It isn't like me to write things down, but when I felt crazy, I used a pack of index cards I brought home from Clark's school supplies, headed each with a date, and wrote down what didn't line up. I hid these from Rose Lee and kept them with a pair of my shoes she wouldn't be caught dead in. Sometimes when she's gone and I'm alone, I spread them out on my bed to get a real good look all at once at what's happening.

One afternoon I spent some time with my index cards and then went to cook dinner for Jeff. I heard a man on the radio say what Alabama's death row was, you sit alone in a hot room until it's time for them to take you out and fry you. Sometimes I worry my life might get like that. What happened was this. Jeff and I were sitting at supper in his kitchen and I was showing my unhappiness by eating almost nothing. He was praising my chicken concoction, and I knew I was getting on his nerves.

He kept urging me to eat, and I kept smiling and picking at my own good cooking. Good cooking was a matter of pride with me although I had no illusions that the way to a man's heart was through his stomach; for the men I knew that would be aiming too high.

He'd worked his way through the chicken and corn and the tossed green salad and had got to the homemade blueberry pie. He was telling me what had happened that day on the construction site, and I was asking the sort of questions that showed I wasn't really paying attention. I kept asking him to repeat ends of sentences and asking him to tell me again who had said what.

I imagined Jeff taking Delia to lunch at the Hill Top, Delia wearing her hot pink mini skirt with red patent leather spike heel sandals, her nails painted a pale green to set off the pink and red. I could see Jeff open the car door for her so he could help her up on the curb, him bending down, enjoying the good view of her legs. Their fingers brush together. Then he watches her sashay after the hostess. I could hear him urge her to have a shrimp cocktail. She dips the jumbo shrimp into the cocktail sauce, tilting her head back slightly as she opens her mouth to eat them with those green-tipped fingers of hers. She leans forward, "Mmm...," she says, "Good." Shrimp! No wonder he's been so willing to take me up on all my offers of home cooking, with him buying Delia jumbo shrimp for lunch.

And all the while I was pushing food from one place on my plate to the other, which is easy enough with chicken and salad but is pretty hard to do with pie. Jeff didn't usually tell me anything much of what had happened during the day so tonight's story must have taken real effort on his part. I supposed he thought hearing about how a load of bricks got moved would take my mind off him and Delia. Or maybe it was a gift to me. I don't know.

He was about to help himself to a second slice of pie and

I was about to get up for some ice cream for him. This wasn't kindness on my part or even habit of setting out to please.

Then Jeff got up and, without a word, went to the cabinet under the sink counter where he kept the pots and bent way in. He came out holding the mouse by its tail, its legs caught on a glue board. I hadn't heard a thing, but I suppose he'd heard a squeak or its tiny little struggle.

I'd had enough of trouble with men in my life to recognize the expression on Jeff's face, so I let out a long wailing "No" and ducked. I didn't hear a splat or thud, what with the sound of my protest, and then I looked up.

Jeff just stood there by the sink, still holding the mouse by its tail. He had a look on his face like he'd been slapped by some stranger. He lifted the lid off the trash and dropped in the mouse.

I listened for its muffled scrabbling. Nothing. I knew enough not to do more than murmur, "I'm sorry." I couldn't ask him, "Why, of all the girls in town, do you have to chase after Rose Lee's best friend? Aren't my friends good enough for you?"

I could tell he wouldn't try to stop me as I left, and I was careful not to slam the door. I was sure I'd be talking to him tomorrow, but judging by his face, he wouldn't be throwing much of anything at me for a while.

If it hadn't been for feeling sorry for the mouse, I suppose what happened could be kind of funny if you have the right sort of sense of humor. Rose Lee wouldn't see the joke in it, and I decided that I'd best not mention what had happened tonight. By the time I'd driven home I'd have some story ready to tell her to explain why I hadn't stayed over. I didn't like to tell outright lies, so I planned to shuffle around until she assumed we'd had a squabble about something unimportant, and I'd come home for some peace. The fact is that my leaving had nothing to do with the mouse. We could have made that up easy enough.

My life is not a movie, and so when I came home, I didn't

expect to find Delia sitting with Rose Lee at my kitchen table, with a half-empty bottle of Jack Daniels for a prop. Rose Lee and Delia had identically painted frosted mauve nails, each with a silver star on the ring finger. The nail polish and the sheet of appliqué nail decorations sat on the table right by the Jack Black. I could tell from the way they held their hands that they'd just done each other's nails.

Rose Lee was looking more like me these days. "Rose Lee," I said, and after just a heart-beat's pause, "Delia."

"Momma," Rose Lee said, not at all apologetic for what she'd brought into our kitchen.

"Pauline," said Delia, smiling like she belonged here without my invitation, sharing my whiskey and my boyfriend with me, sharing a bottle of nail polish with my daughter.

I hadn't been this near to Delia since she'd started seeing Jeff, so I took a hard look at her hennaed hair and her peacock-blue eyes. The story around was she didn't need the contact lenses to see.

"You're home early," said Rose Lee.

"Mmmm," I said. I poured myself two fingers of the whiskey, but I didn't sit down.

"Momma," said Rose Lee, talking just as stern as I'd ever spoke to her, "when will you ever realize that Jeff is a jerk?"

I was glad she'd used the old-fashioned word. Still, I didn't like hearing what she was saying, especially while Delia was listening, though I'd had some thoughts along those lines myself.

I wondered whether Delia or I would defend him, and then I considered what would happen if I dumped mauve nail polish into Delia's hennaed hair, but I wanted Rose Lee to stay at home for a while longer, and an assault on Delia wouldn't help keep her here. I'd have to be on good behavior.

But at least I was going to enjoy telling Janice and Mary Beth about this.

"Pauline," Delia's voice was just the least bit blurred. "I never meant any harm." She looked, for a moment, like a repentant child until her face lit with a grin that reminded me why I'd worried that she'd be a bad influence on Rose Lee. "But then again, to be honest, I never gave it much thought."

I wondered how that could be true when she was with Rose Lee so often and they seemed to be so close, but then maybe some women are born just the same as men, without moral sense, and Delia could be one of them.

"Delia," I said, sitting down, "I'm not sure I want to be having this discussion with you."

"I understand that," she said. "But it can't hurt now. Under the circumstances."

"Your friendship with Rose Lee?" We both looked over at her.

Rose Lee had the grace at last to look embarrassed.

"I didn't mean that, but yes." She paused. "It's just, didn't you know, I'm not seeing him any more."

I did all three of us the favor of not asking how I was supposed to know. "Oh," I said, with the faintest lilt rocking my statement towards a question.

"It wasn't much fun."

Not much fun. I told myself that she was twenty-seven.

"I can't say nothing ever happened." She was almost sulking.

Well, at least she wasn't a liar, too.

"But one thing you ought to know. He never once even mentioned your name."

"Thank you, Delia." Maybe twenty-seven wasn't so young, if she could realize that although he'd slept with her there was one worse betrayal I hadn't suffered. "I am glad to know that."

I supposed Rose Lee could do worse in friends and, after all, I could do still worse in men.

Saturday night that week a crowd was at the Cabin having Clayton's version of a good time. This time last year I was free.

I'd go out to the Cabin with the girls on Friday nights, and sometimes on Saturday, too. And the usual guys would be there to buy us an occasional pitcher and from time to time slide us across the floor. I had no one special like Jeff to make love with, or to cry over. I figure that five years from now I'll still be working at Clark's, coming regular to the Cabin, and I'll watch Jeff do his version of a slow dance, his hips glued to Janice or whoever. And maybe if I'm lucky, some nights instead of coming here I'll stay home and watch TV so Rose Lee and her husband can have a night out.

Jeff picked up his beer and stared down at the ring of water on the varnished table, deliberately replacing the glass several inches away. For some time he didn't look at me, as though what he was doing took all his attention. He drew outward lines from the circle, then, finally, looked up at me and smiled. "Sun," he said, "Sunshine. You are my."

"Am I?" I looked down at what he'd drawn. "Am I really?"

"Sure you are, Sugar." he replied. With the flat of his hand, he swooshed across the sun he had made, so that only a wet smear remained.

I looked over his shoulder across the room to where Delia was sitting with Rose Lee. I caught Delia's eye and winked. She winked back and Rose Lee waved to me and I heard him say, "Really and truly. My one and only. Yesterday, today, tomorrow." He held his hand out across the table and I put mine in his. He traced a soft wet path from my wrist bone to my ring finger and all the way down over its frosted mauve nail where a tiny silver star caught all the light that ever was.

Something To Celebrate

Mary Beth stews over her problems until they fall apart like stringy meat. While she stews she gets cranky, and ragging won't help her case one bit, so rather than wait for Sturge to call her, she'll phone him. She can't be making too much of a mistake by calling him at work unless his doings are common knowledge at the garage. If so, she'll hear it in his voice.

She asks just as smooth and sweet as chocolate milk, "Suppose I cook dinner at your place tonight? I can have it ready by the time you get home."

"What's the rush? I can pick you up on my way home."

He used to be more than happy to have her use her key to get into his house and meet him there. He must have something going on he doesn't want her to know. She doesn't miss a beat. "No rush, Sweet Love, I just thought I'd do something special nice for tonight. On account of it being..." Mary Beth lets her voice trail off like a willow leaf floating downstream.

He'll figure it was one of those anniversaries she was always celebrating with him, anniversaries he couldn't keep track of, like their first movie date, or the first time he'd cooked barbecue, or the first night they'd slept together all night—he'd gotten into trouble missing that one.

Mary Beth has many anniversaries. She believes these little celebrations never grow stale, and with the exception of The Big One, as they call it, she never gives Sturge trouble if he doesn't quite know what they're celebrating unless she tells him, because, often as not, she makes them up. This is the first time she's made one up because she wants something.

"Oh," he says. "Right." He pauses, his tone noncommittal.

"Well, then I guess I'll see you at my place around six. I'll call to see if you want me to pick up anything on the way home."

"Thanks, Sturge. Great." Mary Beth keeps the treacle in her voice, just as if she were planning one of the celebrations. He's so considerate; how could he be running with other women? And why Lila, when he knew it would get back to her, even from Lila herself?

But she knows why Lila. Besides her good-looks, Lila has ways about her, the way she swings her hair, or looks over a coffee cup, or takes the straw out of the Dairy Queen vanilla shake and licks the ice cream off. Mary Beth and her other friends read articles in *Cosmo* to learn tricks like that, but for Lila, they aren't meant to be tricks at all.

Mary Beth's little celebrations are supposed to keep up the romance that is otherwise sure to fade. Big help candlelight has been if Sturge was on the move. "Anything particular you want for supper?"

She always tries to remember to ask, and most often he's content to let her decide; bless him, he'll never fail to comment on how good the dinner is and how pretty she's fixed the table. She's lost count of the number of times he's said the soup she'd made that night was "the best he'd ever eaten." She has to remind herself not to be jealous of her own cooking.

"Dealer's choice."

"You sure?"

"Whatever."

"OK. I'll surprise you." Mary Beth just catches herself from repeating "Whatever?"—which would irritate Sturge, just as his "whatever" has irritated her.

"You always do, Mary Beth, you always do." There was no missing the tone as his voice softens, "Later."

She feels the back of her throat tighten. "Later." She'll miss him. No doubt of that.

In the rain it takes two trips from the car to bring in the

groceries, and, for the first time in months, Mary Beth has trouble unlocking Sturge's door, so when she gets the groceries into the kitchen and the phone rings, she answers it with a sharp edge to her voice, and whoever was on the other end hangs up.

It's nothing for her to answer his phone when he isn't home, just as he answers hers. The phone rings again, and this time Mary Beth lets it go until the machine picks up. She hears the tape click into the greeting message and she turns down the volume so that it's inaudible. She checks the blinking red light; he got two messages before, neither from her. Whoever's on the line goes on and on. She could turn up the volume—after all she turned it down herself—but she believes she'll be better off not hearing. She won't have to play innocent: she will be innocent. Almost.

It's far too soon for Sturge to be on his way home. She makes a quick call to say she's arrived and is just about to start dinner, but she doesn't tell him what happened with the phone.

"You must have got soaked in the rain."

"I'm fine," she lies. "It'll be toasty warm here with the oven on." In her mind she counts to three, then lowers her voice and says, "and I'll be warmer yet when you get home."

"I'm counting on that," he says in a tone so matter of fact that she knows he has a customer.

By six, the phone has rung five more times; each time the caller has hung up leaving no message for Sturge. But for Mary Beth, the message is clear. Some woman is damn eager to reach him, and directly at that.

And by six, Mary Beth has set the table with candles and an African violet brought from her own kitchen window, and put candles on all the tables in the living room. Dinner's about ready, one of Sturge's favorites: chicken baked with apricot jam, green beans and rice-a-roni. There's iceberg lettuce salad with Thousand Island dressing, lots of garlic bread and a frozen home-baked apple pie for dessert. The garlic bread is loaded with garlic, a menu choice aimed at keeping Sturge to herself for a while.

Mary Beth figures the phone situation will take care of itself: the calls will keep coming in, regular, at fifteen-minute intervals until Sturge answers.

The first comes as Sturge is hanging up his jacket. Mary Beth makes no move to get the phone, which, if he'd thought about it, would have struck him as odd. When the machine clicks on, once more the caller hangs up.

"I guess somebody doesn't want to talk to the machine. It can't be real important."

Mary Beth doesn't comment, but busies herself with setting the food out on the table and lighting the candles. When Sturge comes back from washing up he checks the answering machine, noting the messages, but says nothing.

"Don't you want to listen to your messages? I turned the volume down before, so you'll have to turn it back up."

"Why'd you do that?"

"I felt like it. Someone called and hung up when I answered and called right back, and I wasn't up to listening to a message that follows an if-a-woman-answers-hang-up kind of call."

He lets the accusation pass, "Well, suppose it was an emergency or something? Jesus. What's the matter with you?"

Mary Beth smiles and answers, "I suppose if it was an emergency whoever it was would have called back." She isn't about to tell him about the obsessive phoning, or, for that matter, about her lunch with Lila. At least not yet.

"And if you're concerned with an emergency, you could check your messages." She tries hard to keep her voice buttered.

"And ruin this good meal you've worked so hard over? Not a chance."

It would take all of four minutes to check the messages, not enough time to spoil the meal, but time enough to ruin everything else.

When the next call comes, he picks up the phone. He does a lot more listening than talking. His end of the conversation is pretty much a lot of unhnhs and okays, When he comes back to the table, Mary Beth busies her mouth with her food and asks no questions.

"Good dinner, Mary Beth."

"I was hoping you'd like it. I tried to make something you'd like, considering..."

"Considering what?"

"Well, you know...." What she is thinking is, "By tradition last meals are always good."

"Based on all these candles, I'd say we were supposed to be celebrating something special—you've fixed this up pretty. You always were one for romance."

"Were?"

"You know what I mean. Why are you putting words in my mouth, Honey?"

"I didn't mean to." She cut into the chicken. "How was your day? I had lunch with Lila at The Girls' Luncheonette today."

"Yeah, she told me."

"When?" Not like Lila, Mary Beth thinks.

"She stopped in at work after you two had lunch, right before you set up tonight's little so-called celebration."

"Why didn't you say something?"

"What was I supposed to say? That I know Lila told you I took her out. That I expect it to hit the fan because you found out that I kissed her a while."

"A while! She didn't tell me that."

"Well, I'm telling you. Come on, Mary Beth. It's not as though we're in love or anything."

"Was that Lila calling before?"

"I'm not saying anything about that call either."

"And what do you mean, not in love? Who's not in love? You

and Lila—or you and me? What about what you say to me in bed?"

"What am I supposed to say in bed? That I'll love you until I change my mind? That I love you more than I love anybody else, or that I don't love anybody at all?"

"But..."

"Come on. There are certain things a man says. That he has to say. A woman has expectations. And besides, give me a break. It's not as if you love me either."

"What?" The dinner lies on the table between them, the glaze on the chicken congealing like plastic display food.

"Mary Beth. We grew up together. I've known you and your boyfriends from junior high on. George worked with me before he moved, remember? I've seen you in love, and this, as special as you try to make things, is just not it. You haven't heard me complaining, mind you, but who are you trying to kid?"

Mary Beth shifts in her chair. Sturge is right, so much of what she has to think about with him had just happened with George. But with George, the timing had been wrong. For George. At the end they were slow dancing to different tunes. "I'm not trying to kid anybody, Sturge. Just what are you accusing me of anyway?"

"I'm not accusing. I'm just saying that you don't love me. No more than I love you."

"I thought..."

"These candles, the flowers, they're all for...for what? Atmosphere? A great setting?"

"I thought you liked them."

"Well, sure, Mary Beth. And so do you. But face it. You're not in love with me."

"What're you saying? You think I'm just playing house? I'm a little too old to be doing that."

"Right on," he says, "What are you doing?"

"I thought I was doing what you wanted."

"You were. And what you wanted too. But it was like, I don't know, a kind of play—not playing house, but putting on a show of playing house."

"A show? how can you say...."

"Almost as if you pretended enough, got your lines down right, the feelings would follow. Light enough candles, cook the right meals...."

"Make the right moves in bed." Mary Beth's fists are clenched, her nails digging into her palms. Her hands are on either side of her plate.

"That, too. Especially that."

"Well, thanks a lot, so now you're trashing everything. Now that you've decided you don't want me anymore, it makes it easier for you just to say that I never loved you."

"No. I'm saying we didn't, that we don't, love each other."

"That gets you off the hook, doesn't it?"

"I don't have to get off a hook. I'm not on one."

"Oh, please. Now you get righteous."

"It beats the hell out of being self-righteous."

"Thank you. Thank you very much." She pushes her chair back from the table and stands up. She looks down at him, and she walks around the room, turning on the lamps and blowing out the candles, leaving those on the dining room table for last. Soot-filled swirls of smoke rise from the glowing wicks. She doesn't sit down.

He turns in his chair to watch her as she stalks around the room. "Mary Beth. I'm sorry. I didn't intend to get into a nasty fight. I wanted to have a quiet talk about the way things were going..."

"The way they were going? I thought 'things' were going just fine, that we were happy together. Was I wrong?" She waits holding her breath, but Sturge is silent. She knew she was talking too much, but she couldn't stop.

"You were happy, I know you were. I could tell. I was happy.

I wouldn't have been so happy unless things were good for you too. You say you know me. Well, I know you, too...."

"Lila warned me that you wouldn't take this very well."

"You told Lila you were going to dump me before you told me. You're leaving me for Lila. What else did she say to you? I thought she was my friend."

"She—and I never said I was going to dump you. Those are your words."

"What do I know? I thought you and I were...."

"We were what? Name it. You can't. That's just my point."

"What? Do you mean that if it doesn't have a name, it isn't real? That it, whatever it is, isn't important? That I'm not important to you, that you aren't my life?"

She walks over to where he sits. When he touches her arm, she pulls it away. He stands and grabs her wrists, gripping them, her fists still clenched, at her side.

"OK. Things don't need names to be real or important. And you were—still are—important to me. But, no. I am not your life."

"Sturge..."

"I am not your life. I don't want to be. I can't be. No one should."

"But all this time..."

"All this time, all this time, as you put it, is just that—time. A part of your life—and mine. That's all. It's enough."

"Enough?"

"For now. For me there's no more."

Mary Beth looks around. The candles, the violets, her clothes are in drawers and closets; the kitchen is full of her odd plates, serving pieces. "I think I should go home now."

"This isn't about Lila, you know."

"Maybe I'll understand better tomorrow. I'll get my stuff some other time. Let me know when I can pick it up. You have a lot at my place, too."

"We'll work it out."

"It sounds almost as though you were jealous of my past."

"If you believe that, you've missed my whole point."

"The timer's set for the apple pie in the oven. Don't let it burn."

"Mary Beth. You know I'm not just saying to get a life. "

"Walk me to my car, OK. Let's pretend for a few more minutes."

"You have a life . . . And we don't have to pretend. Things don't have to be one way or the other. We can be together. I'm not inviting you to leave my life to make room for Lila or anyone else."

"I'll just take this violet plant. It'll die here before I get it. Don't forget the pie."

"Fuck the pie."

"Fine, you feel that way. Fuck the pie." She crosses to the kitchen, swings open the doors under the sink, grabs the mitts and opens the oven in almost one continuous movement, and reaches in for the pie. She glances at the browning crust as she dumps it into the trashcan under the sink. The hiss and sizzle fill the momentary silence between them. The scent of cinnamon and apple mingles with the garbage that the hot pie scorched.

"You didn't have to do that."

"Don't you tell me what I don't have to do. First you cheat on me and then you try to justify yourself and try to tell me how to live, and then you complain about what I do with a pie that I brought here anyway."

She pulls the trashcan out from under the sink. "Here. You want this after all?" She holds the crushed pie out towards him at arms length, walking towards him. She's still wearing the oven mitts she had given him, so that he faces two green grinning crocodiles gripping the aluminum pie pan dripping coffee grounds. "Nothing says lovin' like somethin' from the oven."

"Give me a break."

"Did you give me a break when you were doing it with Lila or when you were preaching at me before?"

"I never 'did it ' with Lila, I kissed her, that's all. And I wasn't trying to NOT give you a break. I was trying to be honest about what I felt."

"Honest? Wouldn't it have been more honest not to go with another woman and hide it? Now you won't have to worry about what you say in bed—not with me, anyway."

"Mary Beth, I meant it about not wanting to dump you. I did lie about where I was on Monday. I'm sorry for that. I guess I didn't know what to say. I would've told you the truth about it, but I thought you'd be upset . ."

"Upset? Just because you were doing it with one of my so-called friends. OK—'kissing a while'."

"I do want for us to see each other, but not for us to pretend that it's something that..."

"No way in hell I can sleep with you on Saturday and know you slept with someone else on Friday. Or maybe worse—sleep with you Friday knowing you'll be in somebody else's bed the next night."

"Can't or won't?"

"Does it matter? If you say you want to be with me, but you don't want to be my life, then you still have to take into account...." The oven mitts and the remnants of the pie tilt the platter of chicken, a sticky mess all over the cloth.

"I don't have to do anything."

"You don't have to. Right. But..."

"Mary Beth, you wanted me to walk you to your car. You said you wanted me to pretend."

"Not you. I said I wanted *us* to pretend."

"Me. Us. What's the difference?"

"How can you ask that and not say you love me?"

28

"I'm not saying that I don't love you while you love me. I said that we don't love each other. That's all. No more, no less."

"What do you mean when you say "love"?"

"I'm not going to try to explain that. You're not being fair..."

"Fair? I'm not being fair after what you've done..."

"I'm sorry, I'm sorry, I'm sorry. Is that what you want to hear."

"It isn't what I want to hear that matters to me right now. It's what you mean that matters." She looks at the mess of what is left of the dinner. "You want to clean this up?"

"Might as well. We won't be eating it now. No sense letting what can be saved go to waste."

"Waste not, want not. You're full of wisdom, Sturge." Even as she speaks she is sorry. She hadn't intended to let things go so far. Those phone calls had gotten to her. "I don't mean to sound like this. I'm still upset is all."

"I understand. You would be."

She flashes him a look as though the pie might fly through the air like a toaster. "I didn't mean it like that."

Neither of them makes a move to clear the table.

"How did you mean it then?"

"In your eyes I cheated on you."

"In my eyes? How would you feel if I hooked up with one of your friends?"

"There's no sense worrying about it, is there?"

"If you don't understand..."

"I said I did. I said I was sorry. I said I didn't want to end our...whatever you want to call it. You're right about my being jealous; George called the garage the end of last week and I got to thinking, too much I guess, about what'll happen when he moves back."

"George is moving back?"

"When he asked after you, I was worried I'd lose you. I guess my date with Lila was a preemptive strike. It wasn't right to use her for that either."

"And?"

"And what?"

"Can you promise that I won't be hearing any more stories from Lila or anyone else? Well, can you?"

"Lila is your friend. She stopped me from..."

"Wait. She stopped you. And that's supposed to make me feel better?"

"I didn't say it would make you feel better. It's just the way it happened, is all."

"And it won't happen again, right?"

"I already said that."

"No. You didn't. What you said was you don't want to dump me and you're sorry I was hurt, but you haven't committed to anything."

"I won't do anything I wouldn't want you to do. Would you go back to George if he asked?"

"But what if you wouldn't care about my being with somebody else?" She isn't answering his question. She has no desire to wander down that path now. "Would that mean that you'd consider yourself free to screw around?"

"Mary Beth, you're looking for trouble. I can't say let's forget this, but can we at least leave it alone for now?"

"For now. But I've still got to go—at least for tonight."

"If you change your mind, come back. I won't be going anywhere. I'll walk you to the car."

"Don't trouble yourself. I'll be fine."

"Of course you will, but one pie has already gone into the garbage. That's enough waste for one night."

"You're right. But like you said, let's leave it alone for a while." She looks around at the mess she's leaving. The plates of uneaten food and the smashed pie surround her African violet.

"Are you going straight home or are you going to Lila's?"

Mary Beth sighs, surprised at herself when his question

elicits neither suspicion nor irony. "I'm not going to Lila's, but I don't want you to call me tonight."

"Well, OK. But don't forget tomorrow night."

"Tomorrow? What's tomorrow?"

Sturge smiles, his voice honeyed over, "Don't tell me you don't remember—it's our anniversary."

Mary Beth sees he is pleased at his invention, playing her line back to her. "Oh, Sugar..." she murmurs in a voice that sounds as though she means it.

But even before she looks in her rear view mirror at the empty driveway, she knows that in ways having little to do with Lila or with George, she has nothing here that she will choose to celebrate.

She takes the corner fast. She knows what she's doing. She doesn't switch on the radio, but she sings to herself all the way home.

CRUSH

She called herself Lucy. It was only after I had known her for years, after pledging with blood, pinky swears, and sleep-overs where we wore each other's pj's that she told me her name was really Lucretia. We were sitting on her pink-flowered bedspread, and I was holding Mr. Floppy, her favorite stuffed animal, a worn beagle. Her voice was disconsolate, and I hadn't the slightest notion of why she would be distressed. I crooned her name, stretching out all the vowels, ending in "shee-yah."

At the time, I thought Gloria was the most beautiful of all the names I knew, and at my request Lucy was calling me Gloria. Lucretia sounded strange to me, but it was immediately a close second to Gloria as an all-time favorite. But even if it had been number one, I couldn't have asked Lucy to call me Lucretia when that was her name. It would have been too weird.

Even when Lucy explained, I thought it was a beautiful name. She told me the whole story, explained about the Borgia family—the "real" one, she called it. Her family name was Borgia, too. Her name was a joke, she said, like Karen Cutter's family nicknaming her Cookie, or poor Marie Antoinette Jones, whose parents had liked the sound of the name but who were a tad weak in French history. If "they" knew, she warned me, her life would be a misery.

"They" were the rest of the kids in junior high, especially the rowdy boys who tormented our classmate Kay Augustine by chanting, "If you see Kay..."

"What?"

"*If you see Kay.* What will you do—*If You See Kay.*" They said it so that it sounded like they were spelling the F word. And when it was the right time of the month they could make her cry if they teased her enough. Lucky the boys didn't know, but because she took an R day in gym, all of us girls did.

Of course I betrayed Lucy. It was in gym, one of those days when the boys and girls had gym together so we could learn how to dance "civil." The gym teachers weren't much with grammar, but they kept us in line with threats of detention and extra laps around the field or basketball court depending on the weather.

What happened was this. While we were learning to fox trot, Jimmy Fieldstone was running around the perimeter of the court, sometimes veering towards the dancers so they had to jump out of his way. He was doing it to show off, but he only did it when Mr. G's and Mrs. P's backs were turned. I had had a crush on Jimmy since we were in fifth grade and we sat together on the bus trip to the zoo. Girls didn't have to sit with girls or boys with boys, although mostly we did, but Jimmy sat with me and said he liked the way I smelled. It must have been the Cashmere Bouquet soap my mother had just put out. But I didn't tell him, and it was enough for me to like him. He forgot about saying that and pretty much ignored me, but I was stuck on him. He was a convenient crush. Not too much of a JD, but not a goody-goody either. He had his hair in a DA and when he ran laps it kind of fell into his face. I wanted to brush it back over his ears but I didn't know why. I imagined it being damp on my fingers, though, smelling like Vitalis and Old Spice.

Lucy and Michael Longley were dancing on the edge and Lucy could see Jimmy headed right for them. She didn't try to get Michael to move. Instead she let go of Michael and jumped out in front of Jimmy so he crashed into her. I was watching the whole thing and saw her hold her arms out like she was trying to catch someone leaping from a high place. He knocked her down and landed right on top of her, and, before he got up, he kissed her hard on the mouth, and she had her arms around him, with one hand on the back of his head in his wet hair, kissing him back.

Everybody hooted and pointed, but they stayed on the floor like that, Jimmy on top of Lucy like nobody was there until the gym teachers pulled him up by his shirt. Lucy lay there a minute, then got up, crying, but it was too late. All the class was chanting Jimmy and Lucy, Jimmy and Lucy…

Lucy had never kissed anybody like that before—she would have told me. Except in the movie "From Here to Eternity" I'd never seen anybody kiss like that. "I don't know what happened," she said to me—our clothes were hanging on hooks next to one another in the locker room because before that class we used to be best friends. "He kissed me, and it felt…I'm sorry," she said.

She would be sorry all right. She was headed for a week of detention and a note to her parents about her practically having sex in front of the whole gym class. For sure, her father would ground her at least a month. I felt no pity. My body ached with the impact of what I'd seen.

The girls around us were staring and listening to what we said. They might have been hoping she would say what it felt like to kiss like that. "It looked like their mouths were open, too," one of the girls behind me said.

"Are you sorry, LUCRETIA?" I said her real name so loud that Mrs. P marched over to us, with one of her what's-going-on-here-stop-it-right-now expressions slammed on her face. "It's LUCRETIA, Mrs. P," I said, "LUCRETIA started it. You saw what LUCRETIA did in the gym, Mrs. P."

"Well, keep it down," Mrs. P said to me, "Or you'll be keeping Lucy-Lucretia company in detention." And she whirled around, "And the rest of you, too. We have plenty of room."

The bell rang, and the locker room emptied. Lucy followed me out, hissing reproaches as her real name bounced through the crowded hallway ricocheting off the lockers and the green ceiling and walls. But after a few days nobody else cared about her name.

Lucy did have detention. With Jimmy. Her parents grounded her, but she was freed just in time to go to the winter semi-formal with Jimmy. I went alone, which was okay to do. Boys went stag or drag, and the stag boys would sometimes dance with the girls without dates. And girls danced together anyway much of the time with nobody thinking anything about it—though boys, of course, could not dance with each other. Mostly the boys stood in clumps around the walls. Girls sat in the first row of the bleachers or on folding chairs.

I watched Jimmy and Lucy dance cheek to cheek, their bodies pressed together. Her small white wrist was covered by a big white orchid. She had on a pink dress, a new one. When they were fast-dancing near me I stepped out onto the floor, determined to cut in. I could smell the mixture of Old Spice and Jean Nate and orchid, too. It was hard to breathe, and I was afraid to talk because I was sure my voice would squeak.

I reached out and tapped Jimmy on the shoulder. Twice. The first time he ignored me, and with the jitterbug I had to wait for him to come around again. I was sure everyone was staring, because Lucy had stopped sitting with me at lunch and walking with me from class to class. She'd been with Jimmy. I grabbed at his blue jacket sleeve, almost pinching his arm. "I want to cut in," I said. My voice did squeak, but now I didn't care about that.

"No. I want to dance with Lucretia," he said. He said her name as though it were the most beautiful name in the world. "And she wants to dance with me," he said, and, turning to her, asked, "don't you?"

Both of us stared at her. She swallowed hard, but my eyes were filling with tears and they burned with maybe the mascara I was wearing for the first time. She looked at Jimmy and she looked at me, back and forth.

The record changed to Elvis singing, "Are You Lonesome Tonight," which made me cry for real. Lucy and I had practiced slow-dancing to this song in her room. I didn't move. "Well?" Jimmy said, making it a statement that kind of said to me, "Buzz off."

And then Lucy dropped Jimmy's hand and stepped over to me. She put her orchid-covered wrist on my right shoulder. I put my hand in the middle of her back. The pink dress was shiny taffeta, smooth under my palm. I took her right hand in my left. I always led when we danced together. "Lucy," I said. We counted the beats so we could talk but not say in words everything we wanted. We left Jimmy standing on the perimeter as we danced slowly into the center of the gym floor, and we moved together in perfect circles, right out there where everyone could see.

Upstream

Under the sand was something smooth and cool they said was clay. We liked to dig and hold it in our small fists, squish it through our fingers. I wondered how it could be molded into anything. I couldn't believe it would hold a shape. Still it was something to do, finding it. The clay wasn't everywhere, or if it was, we couldn't always reach it. I've never figured that out.

We liked to watch the small schools of minnows and the tadpoles that swam in the shallows. Even though the tadpoles grew legs we never saw any frogs.

The beach was about fifty yards long, Jersey sand. Pines and oaks surrounded the beach, and across the river it was all woods. The river disappeared into woods to the right and to the left. We would have been amazed to see a canoe on our stretch of the river, though it would have had as much right to be there as we did.

The big kids danced in a wooden building, feeding nickels into the jukebox next to a counter where a man sold food. My favorite thing to get was a pretzel stick with yellow mustard for two cents and a dime coke in a bottle that I had to return even though they didn't charge a deposit.

If it rained suddenly, we all ran into the shack and listened to music and the rain on the tin roof, but we hardly ever got caught in the rain. If it wasn't a perfect day, we didn't go there. So almost all I remember is summers of perfect days.

Here the Maurice River ran neither fast nor deep, though it got deeper where it curved out of sight in the woods. We were supposed to stay within sight of the beach, and not head upstream over towards what everyone called Dobie, but I don't know why. When we waded towards Dobie the cedar water came up to my chest and then my neck, and all but once I turned back.

Boys used to climb the trees across from the beach and jump into the water. They didn't dive, of course, just jump, and as far as I know none of them ever got hurt climbing and jumping. We would have heard because it was the sort of place where whatever happened, eventually everyone knew about it even when it was supposed to be a big secret.

Birds. Of course. But most of the time I wasn't conscious of them. They were just part of the beach sound of people talking and the music floating out of the shack. Only once did I ever hear the birds. Marsha Cohen had talked me into going up towards Dobie. I'd turned twelve two weeks before and she was exactly six months younger, but we were in the same grade and were best friends. We walked single file. I went first.

It was July and hot. The cedar water was cool and the riverbed was smooth—even the rocks on the bottom were worn round. When we walked towards the first bend I turned and looked back. The beach wasn't that far away, but it looked like one world in the woods and another in the clearing where everyone was sitting. In the woods we could really hear the birds. I wouldn't say they were singing, just making bird sounds. The only one I recognized to name was a crow and I couldn't see it, just heard it calling from a distance.

The river here was different from the beach, in that here the bank was about a foot above the river, and the water, as I said, came up over the top of my suit and then up to my neck. If the river had been faster, it might have been hard to walk upstream. It would have been easier to go in the other direction, but anyway we knew that going back to the beach would be easier when we went with the current. After we got out of sight of the beach, Marsha said maybe we should go back, but I didn't want to. We argued about it for a while, and I told her it had been her idea so she shouldn't be a baby now, and we kept walking upstream towards Dobie. Once or twice I asked her if she heard voices coming from ahead of us, but she said she didn't. It was my imagination. Marsha walked slower than I did, and she was getting farther behind me the longer we walked. I didn't mind, and I didn't think she did either. I'm sure she never told me to wait up for her or anything else like that.

The trees here reached all the way across the river. We could hardly see the sky, but what we could see was bright blue. The sunlight came through the leaves and made spotlights on the river. The cedar water was so clear we could see our feet. I wished I'd come here before. I liked walking upstream and not talking. It was like being alone but not as scary.

I held my hands out to the side and picked my feet up and let the current carry me back downstream. It was like sitting on the most comfortable chair ever. I floated that way, backwards. I thought I'd bump into Marsha unless she was floating too. But when I turned around she wasn't there. I hollered her name and I thought I heard her say something, but what I don't know. It didn't sound like an echo. I don't know if I was mad or scared or both. But I wasn't going to go back just because she did. I stopped floating and walked upstream again until I got to a place where there was more sun, a sort of clearing, and it was so pretty I forgot to be afraid. Even though I'd been hot before, after walking in the river for a while the sun felt good. I ducked under the water and came up. My hair stuck to my neck and shoulders and I held my face up to the sun.

I let the water carry my weight and I jumped up and down, bobbing for a while in one place, trying not to go back downstream yet. I thought I'd walk just a little farther and then turn back before I got into trouble with my mother. I hoped Marsha wouldn't say where I was. This was her idea.

Up ahead the trees shaded the river again, and I walked looking at my feet because I'd seen a branch under water. I didn't want to get hurt. I figured I'd go just around the next bend to see what was there (more trees probably), though I'd heard of an old farmhouse along here, mostly fallen down. That's what the kids said, though really I didn't know anyone who'd actually been here. I'd give myself about ten minutes at most to get to the bend where I'd turn around. I'd have to guess about the ten minutes because I didn't have a watch.

And then a splash behind me, and as I was turning to see what, shouts and four more jumped out of the trees into the river. They were laughing and calling to one another. At first I was just glad they hadn't landed on me, but then they surrounded me. I didn't recognize them from the beach or anywhere else. They were naked and standing too close to me. One of them said something about my bathing suit and they all laughed. They started grabbing at me and at the straps of my suit. One of them held my hair from behind, so I couldn't move my head. I kicked at them. My fingernails weren't long, and when I tried to slap them, the one whose arm I hit said I wanted to touch him. They tugged at my straps and held my wrists and pulled my bathing suit down to my waist, and they touched me and kept pulling at my suit until it was all the way down, and then they got it off me and tossed it up on the bank and did things to me that hurt, all of them hurting me until they got tired of it and left me standing naked in the river while they climbed up on the bank and put on their clothes, laughing, and ran off into the woods.

I could just reach my suit and got it on and went back downstream, running, pushed by the current right through the spot that had been sunny, but the sun had moved, and it wasn't sunny any more, and I kept going though I hit my leg against the branch and scraped my shin, but I didn't stop, and when I got near the beach a whole bunch of grownups were headed upstream with my mother and Marsha who was crying, too. I didn't want to say what happened in front of everyone, but I told my mother. And she made me go to a doctor probably because I was bleeding for a couple of days, not a period, but bleeding there. And after that things were different.

We didn't go to the beach for the rest of that summer or the next either. Marsha said she was sorry, but, then, after she apologized, she didn't want to see me any more, and I didn't understand why. She hadn't been the one, I had. If it had been the other way around, I would have talked to her. I'm sure I would have. Besides, it would have happened sooner or later anyway. Or something would have. You're a woman, and you know what I mean. After all, even if you never told, you know what happened to you.

No One Can Swim To The Moon

Late May can get hot here, and when it does, we go to the beach at the lake. We'll lie out on the sand like eggs left to hatch. We strip off our tops, lie face down, then flip. We don't much care who sees us, but no one else is there to see, so it's no big deal.

There's a kind of raft that's tied not too far from the shore. When it's hot and the beach is full, that's where we hang out and drink and smoke. It's hard to keep the weed dry, and each year there's at least one screw up, when the bag's not sealed right and then we spread it out to dry on the wood. When it's dry you can't tell it's been in the lake, and it's still good smoke, a nice, clean high.

When I was ten, I'd look at the big kids out on the raft and know that I'd go there too in a few years. I could have reached the raft all right when I was ten, and no sign said how old you had to be to hang out there. But the raft was for teens. Now and then some old man would swim there, grab the edge like he was on his way up to get some sun, and then he'd catch the eye of one of the boys or girls, and let go. He'd make a splash, and then he'd push off the raft and swim back to the beach. No. There was no sign, but we might as well have had one.

This was the last year that I'd be up on the raft. The group of us, who'd hung out all through high school, should have been in class, but we cut to come here. No big thing, just a day off. We'd be done school for good in two weeks. A few hours less there—that's all—and a few more hours here. At least that's how we saw it.

Plan was that we grab some rays, then cook some dogs, have some beer, stay on the beach, play some tunes, you know, smoke, dance on the sand. Hang. In a few weeks it's job time, and some of us will have to leave town to find good work. We set this up last week, with no rain date.

We all left our shoes in a big heap. The floor of the lake near shore is all mud, new pale grass and reeds. Brad and I went to the lake edge to wade, and the mud squished through our toes. We bent to look for the small green frogs. In a month they'll be big and splash and plop and croak. Now they're just cute. I hate the big frogs. When I was a kid I touched one so the boys would leave me be and not tease me.

Brad and I hold hands. We used to date, but now we're friends. Not just friends, you know, but real friends, the kind you can count on. At least I'd like to think so. All of us here are friends, but I guess that in ten years I might not know where they are. It's weird to be so close now and know that some day we won't be.

Mike and Bill are in charge of the fire. They light it when the sun starts to go down. The sun sets right on the lake and the lake lights up all red and pink and clouds streak the sky. It's worth the trip just for that, but of course we're here for more. The food gets burned, but it tastes good like that—you know it's cooked with real fire, not a stove. We've smoked some and the food is like the best thing we've had in years, though of course we kind of know it's not, but I don't know what we would say if we had to swear.

Did I say there's a full moon? Brad points to where it will hang, where it will rise through the woods. The moon looks so big when it's low in the sky. I used to know why. It was the one thing I learned that I thought was cool, and now I don't know it. It makes me sad, to have lost that one cool fact.

Brad starts to throw stones. The guys bet that they can skip the stones more times than the girls, and we get in teams. I try to find the best stones, the flat ones. I used to do this for hours, but that was when I was a kid. I'm still good at it, and I bring up the girls' score so that we pull a tie. The boys want to go one more time, to break the tie, but the girls won't do it. We don't want to lose, but we don't want to win. We like the tie. The guys don't leave it, and keep at us for one more round, and it's not worth the fight. I'm the one who skips for our team, and I go up—with Brad for the guys. I do my best, and we end up with a tie. Brad and I kiss, and it starts as not much, but then it's a real kiss like the ones from the old days, but this one's more, and I don't want the kiss to end, but it does.

They all want to swim out to the raft. It's still warm though the sun is down. I'm not sure. To swim we have to walk through the mud, which was bad in the light. The moon is bright, but not so bright as to let me see what my toes are in. I don't want to stay here on the beach if they're all out on the raft.

We put our clothes with the shoes. We don't fold, we just drop them and run as fast as we can to the lake. Brad and I hold hands, while we run and while we splash through the part of the lake that's not deep and where we wade. But we can't hold hands and swim at the same time, so I drop his hand, or he drops mine, and we're in the lake, and all of us swim and splash our way to the raft.

We sit there on the raft, the old wood worn smooth. There's a chill in the air, and a breeze that comes from the woods. The night air smells like pine and the lake. Jen brought a bag of weed clamped in her teeth, and it's dry and good, and we pass the j. I think that it's too bad we don't have a beer can to use as a bong, but I don't say so. What's the point? Let it seem like the best night we'll have in our lives. I'm scared that it may be, that no night for the rest of my life will be this good, I'm scared that I won't have friends I love this much, and scared that I won't feel this much when I'm old.

The moon spills a path of gold on the lake. I want to slip off the raft, and swim and swim. I want to swim in the gold lake on the gold path till I reach the moon or I drown. I get goose bumps, and I don't know if I'm cold, or if it's that I know that no one can swim to the moon. So I hug Sue and Meg and Jen and all the guys, too, hug them all while I still can, while we're out here on the raft, all of us safe. I have tears in my eyes, and I tell them what I know to be true, that the moon is just a big old stone in the sky.

Where You Want To Go

A few days after I turned sixteen, my mom took me for driving lessons. The driving school was a one-man operation, with a car set up with controls both on the driver's side and on the passenger side. Everyone at high school called the teacher "Mr. P." He was supposed to be pretty good, in that his students all passed the state exam the first time around, even the parallel parking. He'd go with his students to their test, and all the examiners knew him, and called him "Nick," not "Mr. P."

Mom drove to Mr. P's house where he kept the car. Mr. P offered us some iced tea, and said Mrs. P wasn't home. I had heard that there was no Mrs. P, but my mother didn't say no, and we followed him up two cement steps into a cool dark kitchen. I stared at the wood-paneled wall where one of those black clocks that looked like a cat swished a tail back and forth. Mr. P saw me staring and told me that the eyes used to look from left to right and back again, but they'd stopped working the year before, "Keeps good time, though."

He poured two glasses of tea from a yellow pitcher that he took out of the fridge. He put three ice cubes in each of two glasses. He didn't have any himself. "I don't drink and drive," he said, and he winked. Mom laughed, but I didn't see what was funny.

I held on to my glass of iced tea. It didn't have any sugar in it, but I didn't want to ask. The glass was wet with condensation. My hands were already cold from being nervous. I tilted the glass back and forth until the ice cubes made clinking sounds, and when my mother frowned at me I stopped. I shifted my weight from one foot to another, wanting to get to the lesson, but Mom and Mr. P kept on talking. I looked at my legs. They were just beginning to get tan, and I'd shaved them that morning. I wore white socks and sneakers instead of sandals. They looked funny with my shorts, but Mom had insisted, no sandals.

When I looked up, I saw Mr. P staring at my legs. "Sneakers," he said, "good. Better than sandals."

Mom looked pleased. She'd finished her iced tea and stood holding the glass with the melting ice cubes.

"OK, now," Mr. P said, "OK." He took Mom's glass from her and set it on the table, then held his hand out for my glass. "Not much for iced tea, are you? That's OK. It's an acquired taste." He paused and then he winked at Mom again. "Lots of things are, isn't that right, Mrs. Ricci?"

Mom didn't laugh. She shrugged, the way she shrugged at home when she didn't want to talk about something, but she didn't want to start a fight either.

Mr. P set our glasses on the counter next to the sink. I thought he could just as well have put them in the sink, but I knew it would be rude to say anything.

Mr. P told mom that when the lesson was over he'd drive me home. And then he stood, leaning against the counter where he'd put the glasses, until Mom offered to pay him. "OK," he said, "OK now, that doesn't have to be now."

Mom closed her purse, and he added, "But if you want to, that's OK. Now or later it doesn't matter. Now is good."

I hoped his driving lessons would be easier to understand, but my mom understood and gave him a check, which he put on the table under the sugar bowl, "so it doesn't blow away." That was supposed to be another joke because there was no breeze at all, not in the yard, not in the kitchen.

We all went out into the yard, and Mr. P showed us the car and explained the two sets of controls. He must have given this introduction hundreds of times, but it didn't sound like a memorized speech. He went on and on, and though he didn't say it exactly, he let us know that he was really proud of the car.

The two sets of controls were a big selling point for his lessons. The car had a big sign on top of the roof, "STUDENT DRIVER." I remembered Dad joking when he saw that sign. Now people would be laughing at me.

"OK," Mr. P said, "OK now, Let's take this show on the road." He laughed at his joke and I wondered if he said it before every first lesson. He opened the door for me and made an exaggerated bow.

Before I could get into the car Mom put her arms around me and gave me as big a hug as though I were moving to China or going to Girl Scout Camp. "My baby's not a baby anymore," she said.

"I'm not a baby," I thought. I didn't see what the big deal was, anyway. Every girl I knew learned how to drive. Still, I was nervous, and learning to drive was important, but not the sort of important for a hug like the one I was getting.

Mr. P didn't say anything, but instead of waiting for me to get into the car and closing the door for me, he walked around to the other side and got in, pulling his door shut pretty hard, just shy of slamming it. He leaned towards the driver's side where I was still standing outside being hugged, "OK," he said, "OK now. Let's take this show on the road." This time he didn't laugh.

I got into the car and pulled the door shut. The window was down, and I waved and smiled at my mother. I couldn't believe she was actually wiping away a tear.

I wondered who would drive away first. Then I realized that Mr. P wasn't going anywhere until my mom pulled out of the driveway.

The sun felt hot on my bare thighs. Either Mr. P's car had no air conditioning or it was broken. Mr. P reached into his shirt pocket and pulled out a pack of chewing gum. He pulled out a stick and unwrapped it. "Quit smoking," he explained. He held the pack out to me, "Bet you can drive and chew gum at the same time," he said. He laughed.

I knew this was supposed to be a joke. I didn't think it was so funny, but I wanted to be polite, so I smiled. Still I didn't want the gum. "No thanks, Mr. P," I said.

"Call me Nick," he said. "OK, OK now? Nick."

As far as I knew, the only people who called Mr. P "Nick" were the men at the Driver's Examination. Even with the car windows down I could smell the Juicy Fruit Chewing Gum and an aftershave I knew was English Leather. There was another smell in the car, too, but I didn't recognize it. I was just glad the windows were open.

I smiled and nodded, but I didn't use his name. "Let's get this show on the road," I said, hoping he would like it if I used his exact words. I didn't want to make him mad when we were just starting.

Mr. P turned toward me. "OK, OK now, you look at me and see how my hands are on the steering wheel. "We call this position, ten and two, like the hands on a clock."

His hands gripped the wheel. He wore a yellow polo shirt, and his arms were covered with curly dark hair. Even his fingers had hair on the knuckles. Dark hair curled out of the V of his open collar. I hadn't noticed before.

"Put your hands on the steering wheel, ten and two," he said.

I followed his instruction, but he shook his head, and placed his hand over my right hand and moved it down the wheel. "Not at one, at two."

I was afraid he was going to reach across my body and move my other hand, too. He couldn't do that without brushing against my chest. But he just said, "Move your left hand down a couple of inches, kiddo."

He told me how to use the pedals, went on about signals, mirrors, all the things I had in driver's ed. He even gave "the instrument of death" speech about driving. I wondered who'd started that speech, thinking that it was a pretty stupid idea.

"OK, OK now. Let's get this show on the road," he said. "Check your gear, turn the key, give it some gas, and don't forget to steer."

I rolled out of his driveway. I was glad he lived in the country and that there wasn't much traffic here, so I didn't have to start by backing out into the road. He must have read my mind because he said that next time we'd practice backing. His saying "we'll practice" instead of "you'll practice" was right out of the driving teacher's handbook.

He explained how one principle was to keep your eyes where you want to go, not where you don't want to go. It sounded like he was telling me how to live, not how to drive, but I knew he was just talking about the road. He sounded like a preacher when he said it, as though it was the most important thing in the world. It was kind of tricky, too, like telling you not to think about a purple cow.

The road was deserted at this time of day, so I didn't have to worry about traffic, just maintaining a steady speed and staying in lane. After a while I glanced over at him and he was staring at me. I thought with his controls and all, he'd be watching the road. His hands weren't on his steering wheel either.

"Keep your eyes on the road, OK," he said. "On the road, OK now, and where you want to go, not where you don't. Look at the road, not at the big trees along side the road."

His right arm rested on his door in the space of the open window. His left arm stretched out so that it was on the top of my seat.

Even though while we were moving, a breeze came in the window, I could still smell his aftershave and that other smell I didn't know.

"Your hair is in your eyes," he said.

It was, too, the wind had blown it there. I hadn't thought of that when I combed my hair. I could have put it in a ponytail.

"That's a distraction from driving, kiddo," he said.

I lifted my hand from the wheel. "Keep your hands on the wheel." He leaned over and brushed his fingertips, over my face, tucking the hair behind my ear. "That's better, isn't it?" he asked. His voice was soft. It didn't sound anything like the driving lesson.

Before I could answer, I saw a yellow jacket flying around in the front of the car. It flew up and bumped against the inside of the windshield. I don't mind honeybees, but I don't like yellow jackets. They're mean.

I tried to keep my eyes on the road, but I also watched the yellow jacket. I wondered what Mr. P would do about the yellow jacket. Mr. P kept his hand on the back of my seat. I thought I felt his fingers on the side of my neck. The yellow jacket circled down and landed on my thigh. I was still driving, but slower.

I kept my eyes on the road, the yellow jacket on my thigh, so light that if I hadn't seen it land I might not have felt the slightest tickle of its feet landing. And Mr. P hadn't moved his hand, I was sure. It was probably my imagination, thinking his hand was on my neck. He probably hadn't noticed the yellow jacket on my thigh. I didn't want his hand on my thigh. And I kept my eyes mostly on the road, knowing that I was going to be stung. It hurt, but I knew I had to keep control of the car, no matter what. Eyes where I wanted to go, not where I didn't.

I pulled over real slow onto the sandy shoulder of the road and stopped. I smacked the yellow jacket, squishing it dead, my open palm slapping my thigh with a sharp sound. Mr. P gave a long low whistle. His breath still smelled like the sweet gum, and with the car stopped, his aftershave and that other smell made me dizzy. Or maybe it was the heat. I flicked the dead insect off my thigh. It hit the ashtray and fell to the floor. My hands were shaking.

"I think it's time to go home," I said. "I think this lesson is over." I leaned forward and turned on the radio to the rock station I liked. It was news now, and I didn't want to sit through it so I turned it off. I knew I was being rude and I didn't care. He wouldn't dare say anything bad to my mother. If I felt like it later, maybe I'd tell on him. My leg hurt where I'd been stung.

"Let's take this show on the road," I said, not wanting to please him, but for the fun of it. I'd put baking soda or something on the sting when I got home.

Mr. P looked at his watch and at the dashboard clock. "OK," he said, "OK now. Let's take this show on the road." I wondered if he'd heard me, whether he knew what he was saying or whether it was all habit, even his arm across the back of my seat. Then he added, "Think you can do a U turn here? I nodded, looked both ways, and turned the car. I leaned on the gas pedal, and as I drove, the air from the pinewoods filled the car. I went the limit all the way home, never looking again even once at all the places I didn't want to go.

THE RED TIGER

1. The Red Tiger

D avis lay awake listening. He listened to the jungle night birds, and thought about how different they were from the rhythmic thuk-thuk-thuk-thuk-thuk of the copters the men called birds, too. He wondered if all the calls were really birds, or signals. They did that, he'd heard.

The men were sleeping, and in the two hours since they'd sacked out their breathing had synchronized. Only Harris' snoring was off, and now and then he'd talk in his sleep. Clark was on guard duty. Davis did not have to be awake.

When he got home, he thought, it would be a long time before he'd want to walk in the rain or go camping again.

He opened his eyes and stared up towards the leaves. Without the moon he could see neither sky nor leaves. Canopy, he thought, remembering the layers of bright green that he could not see in the dark. He would have liked the luxury of looking at the patterns of leaves, or listening to the sounds without thinking about what they might be, without listening for a twig cracking or a burst of fire.

He did not want to desire anything. To have desire, he recalled, it was necessary to experience a sense of deprivation. He could not afford the luxury of desire.

Davis could empty himself of all earthly desires. For weeks Harris had been talking about it, saying he was "empty of all earthly desires." The men had laughed at him because Harris talked in his sleep. He had not rid himself of desires, they told him, quoting his sleep-talking at length. Harris had turned red, then shrugged. Davis told the men to knock it off.

Canopy, he whispered, thinking of a red-and-white-striped awning in his in-laws' back yard, of white flowers in vases and tall tropical trees imported for the day in pots that men carted away at the end of the party.

His little sister Carrie had read him a poem about a red tiger. It had nothing to do with the wedding, but she had read it to him anyway. It was a poem she said she'd written for school.

He'd said there were no red tigers, and if there were, what color would their stripes be?

"Red tigers don't have stripes," she'd answered

"Then how do you know they're tigers?" he asked.

"You just know," she'd said as though it were something important, something he should remember. "They're very dangerous, and they pounce just as you're falling asleep."

"How do you know?" he'd asked again. He was annoyed with himself for being so aggressive, but he kept pushing her anyway.

"You know. You look into their eyes just before you die," she kicked a clump of grass. "Everyone they pounce on dies."

"Then how do you know they exist if no one is left to describe them?"

"You just know," she said again. She kicked at the lawn again. "You ask too many questions. Didn't you ever hear about poetic license?"

"So red tigers are poetic license?" He was beginning to feel like a bully, but he kept on, "They're not real after all?"

Julie walked over, carrying two mugs of coffee. She was still wearing shorts and a tee shirt. The ceremony wouldn't be for hours. She handed him a mug of coffee.

"I thought it was bad luck to see you before the wedding?" he said.

"Silly," Julie put her arm around his waist. "I want to see you all I can."

"Julie," Carrie said, "Make him believe me. He doesn't

believe me about the red tigers."

Julie smiled. "I don't like the red tigers, Carrie. They scare me."

"You should be scared. They're very dangerous." Carrie turned towards the house. "I'm going to get more breakfast, she said, over her shoulder. "Their eyes glow in the dark. You can see their eyes coming towards you even when it's too dark to see anything else. When they pounce, their eyes are the last thing you see."

Davis lay still, awake, listening to the birds in the trees he could not see. It was too dark to see anything really. He lay awake watching.

2. Sister

At the end of the wooden dock, Jewel sat in last year's faded blue bathing suit, a blue plaid shirt beside her. She dangled her legs, scissoring the air above the lake. From time to time she'd lean forward to look for the little fish that swam among the pilings and bit if you held still but didn't if you kept moving.

From way out on the lake Jewel heard the wail of a loon and just caught sight of its checkered back before it dived. She wondered why it was hiding, how long it would stay under. It was the sort of thing Lane knew and would tell her if he were still here.

Jewel spread Lane's soft shirt across her lap. He'd let her have it, as a loan, he'd said, before he left for boot camp.

The edge of the dock cut into her legs, and when she stood up there'd be a red line across the back of her thighs that itched and burned at the same time.

She'd wait and watch for the loon to come back, to see its black head break the surface of the lake. She knew if she waited long enough and looked hard enough she'd find the loon. She was sure of it. The loon would resurface somewhere. It would, she was sure.

3. Jewel

My little sister Carrie thinks she's so special. Everyone in the family tells her that she's going to grow up and be a famous writer. She writes poems about things she imagines, like red tigers, and she makes you listen to them.

My name is Jewel, and I am not a writer. But I like to look at things and think about them. And I write down what I see and think.

My brother went to war right after he got married to Julie. Our names are almost alike, Jewel and Julie. Isn't that funny? Julie's nice, and sometimes when we're together she gives me a big hug for no reason at all, and then I know she's thinking about my brother and missing him.

The War is on television every night. The reporters are over in Vietnam taking picture of lots of what's going on. My dad said that in World War II there were newsreels that showed at the movies along with the features. One theater in Philadelphia, which is the biggest city near here, showed nothing but these newsreels. They weren't even in color. That's a part of history, too.

We try not to be having dinner at the same time we watch the news. My little sister has to leave the room because she's not supposed to be watching the news. She did one night, and she asked Dad about the body count.

Our brother Lane sends us letters, all of them addressed exactly alike: The Davis Family, and then our names. One of them asked me if I was taking good care of his shirt. I have to give it back when he comes home. Carrie got one, too.

Most nights I sleep with the shirt. When I was even younger

than Carrie, I had a blanket that I liked. This shirt isn't anything like that.

Once I came into my room and Julie was sitting on my bed. She was smelling the shirt. I looked at her and said, "Mom washed it by mistake. She didn't know that I didn't want her to."

Julie held the blue plaid shirt in her lap, her fingers wound up in the soft flannel. Sometimes she cries when she thinks that no one is looking, but she wasn't then. Although her name is on the letters to the Davis family, she always gets her own letter, too.

Last summer while we were in Maine, there were riots in Chicago. Some people called them demonstrations. We learned about the Bill of Rights in school. Still, I wish they wouldn't. Lane asked in his letters about what was going on in Philadelphia in the anti-war movement.

Four years ago there was an anti-war demonstration in Rittenhouse Square. I was really young then, but I remember it because it was the first one and Dad and Lane talked about it a couple of nights in a row.

In my letters I didn't tell Lane how angry some of the kids in school are about the war. They say that if they have to go to Vietnam they won't go, but they'll run away to Canada, and some of them say that their parents have promised to buy them the ticket.

Dad says that when these people grow up they'll be nostalgic about protests and marches. He asked if I knew what nostalgia was. Sure. It was one of our vocabulary words in English.

I wonder if Lane has time to be nostalgic about our summers in Maine. We go to the lake every day. Our house has a long lawn and then there's a path down to the lake.

Loons are on the lake, and we like to watch them. Carrie and I try to guess where the loon will come up after it dives. We make it into a game to see who'll be right. We even keep score. Lane used to play that game with us, and he'd tell us

Nature Facts. He wants to teach biology in a college when he gets home. He'll be good at that.

My brother Lane is a target. Today kids at school were talking about something they called fragging. I couldn't listen long because I'm worried about Lane. I think fragging is murder.

In a way it's funny to think about murder happening during a war. Where is the line? Killing some one on your own side is wrong. I would have trouble killing anybody, and I hope Lane doesn't. But he might have to.

4. Carrie

Everything is political: the personal is political. When my big brother Lane went to Vietnam, even though I was too young to realize it at the time, I was politicized. I realized that by the time I grew up, the war would be history, so I decided that I would teach history. I wanted people to understand how things were. I still do.

Lane left for Nam right after he married Julie. He'd signed up for R.O.T.C. and pretty much knew that he'd be going there. And then again there was the draft lottery anyway.

He gave one of his flannel shirts to Jewel and another favorite shirt to me. I liked to carry it around, and I slept with it. Once when Jewel wasn't looking, I took the shirt he'd given her to see if I liked it better than mine, but I put it back before she knew it was gone.

New York is not Chicago, and the demonstrations in New York last summer were nothing like the demonstrations in Chicago in 1968. I didn't go to either. I was too young to go to Chicago, and too cynical to go to New York.

Even though I didn't go to New York, I did vote. My husband Rob and I take our daughter, Lily, to the polls so she sees that it's important. Rob and I also have a son we named Lane after my brother. Lane didn't go with us this year—he's in the Army, Iraq.

Our son grew up hearing about his Uncle's blue shirt, and before he left he gave Lily one of his shirts—lent her his blue shirt. You wouldn't think he'd be sentimental like that, but he's a good kid.

Our family has voting traditions. After we vote Rob and I meet up with my family, and we all have dinner together and watch TV until about midnight. Then on Wednesday we have dinner again and go over the whole thing, listen to the talking heads on cable. We switch around from channel to channel. Each year the production values change, but, basically, it's the slow grind of the electoral college on the vote.

In 2000 I thought we'd be having dinner together the whole year because of the Florida debacle. That was an unnecessary circus. And depending on what your politics are you decide who's the clown.

Rob and I read *the New York Times* on Sunday, and we watch C-Span. We think of ourselves as independent.

I asked Lane what he thought about the Swift Boat Vets and Kerry. He put his hands over his ears, then over both eyes, then over his mouth—the three monkeys, See No Evil, Hear No Evil, Speak No Evil. Then he winked and reminded me that the three advisors were monkeys.

I'm glad I have those photos of myself in mini-skirts. It keeps me from freaking out entirely when Lily takes swatches of fabric off the rack and says that's the skirt she's been looking for.

When she wears her brother's shirt with her skirts, the shirt is as long as the skirt. Oh well, most of the time she wears jeans. The jeans she chooses aren't the ones that show her belly button, though some of her friends wear those low-rise jeans with little tee shirts that bare their midriffs, even in winter.

I try to remember that we wore miniskirts, hip huggers, bras optional, and we weren't all sluts. I try to stay non-judgmental about this fashion thing, but I'm glad that the fad is over for those tee shirts that said things like "slut" or "easy" or "candy." So far Lily hasn't mentioned tattoos or piercing anything other than her ears.

When she turns fourteen in June, I'll take her to get her ears pierced and she can pick out some earrings for a birthday present. But no nose ring, eyebrow ring, navel ring, etc. I can be such a prude!

This year we'll take one of her friends up with us when we go to the lake in Maine. Our family still has the house there, and we all go up in the summer. When I see Lily sitting on the end of the dock, it brings back the memories I have of sitting there, guessing about where a diving loon would resurface. Sometimes I sit there with Lily, and we talk about what she'd call "stuff."

She spent a lot of time with Rob and me in the den while we watched the war news when the embedded journalists were still sending their reports. Lane is there now, and I know something about what she must be feeling. I try to give her the opportunity to talk about it by talking about how I felt when her Uncle was in Nam.

She really looks up to him. And now I understand how tough it must have been for Mom not to let me know how worried she was when he was in Nam.

"Mom," Lily said, "please tell me again about the red tiger." She looked up from her spiral-bound notebook that lay open on the kitchen table.

She likes to start her homework essays in handwriting before she uses the computer. She has an assignment to write about some aspect of family mythology.

"I'm not sure the red tiger fits the assignment," I said. Immediately I was sorry. My words couldn't have been better chosen to annoy a teenager. I apologized while she was still wailing, "Mom."

"I have to write about family stories and myths. 'Specially a significant one." She dropped the pencil eraser straight down so it bounced on the Formica tabletop. She caught it and dropped it again. Each time she held the pencil up higher, and it bounced higher.

This would be a fine physics experiment; I shuddered thinking about the upcoming Science Fair. I hoped this year's experiment wouldn't involve rotting fruit. Or gerbils.

"The red tiger is very significant in our family, Mom. Uncle Lane talks about it all the time." She paused. "Well, not all the time, but lots, anyway."

She was right, and I wasn't actually positive what Mrs. Ellis means when she talks about family mythology, anyway. One year the classes worked on a joint project, history and English, using documents and artifacts as an indication of family history. She'd probably like a poem being significant in a family story.

"I need to know about the how the red tiger affected the wedding. I'm going to talk to Aunt Julie and Uncle Lane tonight. I'm supposed to bring together "different narratives." She took a deep breath, then added, "To reconcile inconsistencies.""

She held out a piece of paper so I could read it. Yup. That's what it said.

"You get to go first," she said.

"There's not much to tell, Lily." I said, "Uncle Lane and Aunt Julie were getting married at her parents' house. On the back lawn. It was early in the day before any of the guests had arrived, but preparations were in full swing A big tent with folding chairs, and so on."

"Where was the tiger?"

"The tiger was in a poem I wrote in school, that's all. There was no real tiger."

"I know," she said, "it was a red tiger." Her voice changed, "Where was the red tiger at the wedding? What was so dangerous?"

"I imagined the tiger," I said, "The tiger itself was dangerous."
I paused. "I think I must have been upset about Lane leaving to
go to the war."

"And getting married,"

"Oh, probably not,"

"Probably yes," she said. "I want my brother to be happy, but
I know that when he gets married, it will change everything."

"I was in the wedding," I said, surprised at the petulance in
my voice. "I had a frilly pink lace dress and a big satin bow."

Lily wrinkled her nose, "You liked that?"

I laughed. I never wear frilly clothes now. A warning voice
whispered to me. "I wasn't the frilly type, but I liked Julie."

"Julie's cool," Lily said.

"It was just a poem I wrote. The tiger would pounce. Its eyes
were the last thing you saw before you died."

"Creepy," she said, "and a little weird for a wedding day—
especially before Uncle Lane goes to war."

"It was weird," I admitted. Lane said he'd thought about the
red tiger the whole time he was at war.

He'd mention it even now when something bad was
happening. "Is that a tiger's breath I smell?" he'd say.

I guess it was a myth, kind of. "They're quiet and sneaky,
these red tigers," I added.

"Oh, when did 'the' red tiger become 'they'?"

"I don't know," I said, although I did, in fact, know, to the
day. "If you want me to, I'll look to see if I can find the poem."

"Awesome," Lily said. "I don't know why I didn't think of
that." She bent over her notebook and started writing.

I went, but I knew already what I would find, four corner
holders and a pale space in the scrapbook where the paper had
been. I had torn it up myself.

When Lane said he'd got his orders to go to Iraq I'd found
my scrapbook and turned to the page where the poem had been

pasted by my parents. I re-read the poem, and I can visualize the page still, wide blue lines and dark pencil with careful printing on yellowing brittle paper.

I pulled it out and tore it into tiny pieces, put them in a big plate and burned them. The volume was surprisingly small. I mixed the ashes into a meatloaf and served it up for dinner. I didn't tell Lily or Rob what I had done. I thought I'd understood the concept of devouring your enemy's heart.

What I hadn't considered was that by eating the tiger I had made it a part of myself. And although they didn't know it, now Lily and Rob had the red tiger within them, too.

I went back into the kitchen. Lily looked up from her work and frowned. "No luck?"

"It wasn't there," I said, conscious of the deception. "But you have everything, don't you?"

"I'll be fine," she said.

I knew that she would. Tonight her Uncle and Aunt would tell her their stories. Lane might tell her about his nights in the jungle in Nam, while my son is making his way across another alien landscape.

On the evening news we see dark smoke rising from a metal carcass, victim of an I.E.D. I look at my husband and daughter, serious, intent, watching. I am restless. The red tiger paces. These days I avoid mirrors, afraid I will recognize, reflected, what I still fear most to find, the red tiger's wide gold eyes.

Secret

A thin film of coffee covers the bottom of the carafe, which, as a courtesy, her houseguests, the Blumenthals, have left on "warm." Judith pours the scorched liquid into the sink, and opens the freezer to take out the coffee beans, which have been disappearing so quickly that she might as well have had them ground at the store. She starts a new pot. She has forgotten how much other people consume.

Today this set of other people will go home to White Plains. Her college roommate, Eva, and Eva's husband, Leonard, and their teenage son, Alan Michael, will leave her Swarthmore house for what Eva called "their little nest."

Although the Blumenthals had been making visits for almost twenty-five years, this is the first year Judith feels she has suffered an infestation. Something terrible has happened to Eva, she is sure, in the two years since the last visit, some short circuit in her brain's wiring, or maybe her synapses have been wired together to change the way Eva uses language. Instead of saying, "Can I give you a hand with dinner?" she examines every possible aspect of dinner preparation and how she can figure in its production. Plans for the day are similarly explored, in a way that Judith thinks of as pointillist perseveration. She looks at her old friend transmogrified and asks herself, "Is this The Change? What's happening to *me*?"

A voice at her side interrupts her reverie. "Judith, dear, my Leonard made coffee this morning, but my Alan Michael had three cups before he went running. Did I tell you my Alan Michael runs three miles every morning, Judith dear?" Alan Michael has run each day they've been there, so this is the eighth time Eva has told her, using, Judith thinks, nearly the same words. She knows what will come next.

"I think he shouldn't run in this heat in spite of his being in training and trying to lose weight to make the 137-pound-weight class for wrestling, but My Leonard says that my Alan Michael is getting to be a man, and men...." Eva speaks a little too loudly, talking over the voices of talk radio, a station strange to Judith, who keeps her radios set to classical music stations.

The Blumenthals changed the station almost before they had set down their bags. They'd explained to Judith that they kept talk radio on at home "to find out what real people think." Eva said that since Leonard had retired early from his business as an accountant, "he's taken such an interest in the real world."

They'd reminded her assertively that she, Judith, had told them that they should always think of this as being their home away from home. Of this Judith has no memory, but her memory is not what it used to be. She'd look for something and forget what she was looking for. And names vanished and reappeared: names of former students, and names of what she thought of as new actors. The only actor's name she could remember was Jean-Claude Van Damme, and she didn't know what he looked like or the title of a single one of his films. Judith tunes back into the conversation: Eva is crooning that she "was sure you wouldn't mind, would you, Judith dear? You know what My Leonard says."

Judith feels herself raising her voice to ask about what Leonard says, but just then he walks into the kitchen, carrying an empty coffee mug, and beams at Judith, who has poured herself a cup of the coffee she's made. "I see you found the coffee I brewed," he says.

"My Leonard is so helpful around the house, aren't you Leonard, dear? I hope my Alan Michael will make some woman as happy as you've made me, Leonard dear."

Judith believes he will. She has watched him grow from a sandy-haired tot sucking on a pacifier to a seventeen-year-old who rarely appears without headphones attached to a CD player on so loud that when they are three feet apart she hears the *chkk chkk chkk* of the music. He's at the awkward stage, and on the second day, he shorted out the microwave when he knocked over a cup of coffee he was trying to reheat.

Leonard smiles absently. Perhaps he's tuning his attention to the discussion on the radio. Perhaps the voices on the radio and on TV represent a clever skirmish in Leonard's war against Eva's new onslaught of words? "I'm a lucky man," he says as he returns to the living room where he sits all day reading the *Times* and listening to C-Span. Sometimes when Judith walks through the room, Leonard looks up and swears in a gentle, old fashioned way about an amendment he feels is "downright wicked." He vows to vote Libertarian or Unitarian, which Judith recognizes as his political and religious humor.

What have she and Eva been talking about during their weekly phone calls? Has someone substituted an Eva-look-alike for her friend? "My Leonard listens to talk radio all night. Did you know that, Judith dear?" Eva nods solemnly and confesses, "I wear ear-plugs. . ."

Judith does know that he has the radio on all night. She can hear it through the wall. "Is this something new?"

"He started last year when I had the hot flashes and woke him up when I threw off the covers. My Leonard was so understanding, but to fall back asleep he turned on the radio and that's how it began." Eva sighs, "You know how it is?" Eva keeps talking about The Change and her new gynecologist, and her old doctor, and physicians' assistants and "how helpful" and "how kind," "how dear".

Judith hears Eva's voice and the radio on the counter and the television and she swears that she can hear the radio from the guest room still on and even, yes, a radio in her study which Alan Michael has been using as, he would say, "a place to crash." The air is thick with words like gray moth wings, making her blink as the moths fly too close to her eyes, beating against her exposed flesh. She wants to scream and put her hands over her ears, but if she does, they'll fly into her mouth. This is crazy, so instead she pours too much cleanser into the sink and scrubs.

"Judith dear, do you still write your cute poems?I haven't seen you writing at all the whole time we've been here. I always thought your poems were so cute, even back in college..."

Judith wants to grab Eva by the hair and stuff the can of Comet into her mouth, but she knows Eva does not consider "cute" an insult. Judith thinks her own poems are cute like Albert Pinkham Ryder's paintings are like Holly Hobbie illustrations. "Well, Eva, I've been spending all my time with you. And about the poems, I'm not exactly trying to be cute." She is careful to keep her voice under control.

"But you rhyme, and your poems look so nice on the page, Judith dear, and you write about nature so well, naming all those little white flowers. And we'll be gone in a few hours and then you can write to your heart's content. You write little stories now, too, don't you? I was always so proud of you, Judith dear, you know that..."

Judith does know, and she can hear the hurt in her friend's voice. What was it Anais Nin said, "We don't see things as they are, we see things as we are"? Eva sees cute. She herself sees infestations. And so, when Eva asks Judith about her social life, instead of side-stepping the question, Eva stares hard at the calendar on the fridge, her appointment with her gynecologist, Dr. Roitman, on the 28th. She decides to let Eva have something to fuss over.

"He's like a comet the way he came into my life. A momentary streak of light in my sky."

"Who is he? How did you meet him? What does he do?" Delight wars with concern in Eva's voice.

Judith forestalls more of what will be a long series of questions by interrupting with a partial answer. She smiles and says, "His name is Jean-Claude." Judith turns to get another cup of coffee and Eva waves away the offer of yet another cup.

"What a romantic name!"

"We met three months ago in Border's on the Main Line. We were both reaching for Mary Oliver's poems." Judith continues before Eva can ask about Mary Oliver. "He teaches English too."

"And you both like poetry! You have so much in common, why a comet and not some other heavenly body, like the sun, maybe?" Judith smiles at her friend's unwitting pun, but Eva continues, "Don't have such a negative attitude, Judith dear. Just because you haven't been so lucky as I was with my Leonard. He isn't one of those men of yours who...?"

"He's just young. That first night when we had coffee he said he liked older women. What he said, exactly, was, 'Who would you rather talk to, a girl nineteen or an older woman—twenty-nine?' And I thought, older, twenty-nine!"

"But, Judith dear, you must be old enough to be his mother."

"I'd rather think that he is young enough to be my son."

"I don't see the difference."

"I do. Listen. I always asked, "How old were you in 1968? to help me figure out what somebody'd think. He wasn't even born."

"Judith dear!"

"When I talk about something that happened before he was born—which isn't such a good idea in a situation like this—he asks me if I know where he was then? And I say no," Judith pauses, but continues before Eva can interrupt. "And then he says he was waiting to be with me. We celebrated his twenty-eighth birthday together."

"That *is* romantic, Judith dear. It reminds me of my Leonard, who when we were dating said the nicest things, and he still does, and he's so considerate. He always helps around the house and he always praises my baking, you know I love to bake, and I wish I had brought you some of my *schnecken*, but you were always such a good baker, too, Judith dear. Did you make this Jean-Paul of yours a birthday cake?"

"Jean-Claude. Why does everybody say Jean-Paul?"

"Jean-Claude, I'm sorry, of course, Jean-Claude, but did you make Jean-Claude," she emphasizes the second syllable now each time she says his name, "one of your wonderful carrot cakes?"

"No." Judith lowers her voice, "Eva, when I asked what kind of cake he wanted he said he didn't want a cake. And when I asked what he'd put his candles on, he said, 'I'll put them on your body.'"

"Your body?"

"We used tea lights. Not twenty-eight. But I lay very still and he placed the tea lights just so, and lit them."

"Weren't you afraid? And fire!"

"And when they were all lit I asked him if he made his wish."

"Judith dear, you didn't."

"Eva dear, I did." Judith thinks about lying in the dark, on her bed, naked and motionless with tea lights on her chest and belly and thighs, and her Jean-Claude looking down at her candle-lit body, as she looks up at his candle-lit face. And then she can almost feel his breath on her body as he blows out the candles. She smiles, glowing with the secret pleasure of the moment.

"Remember, he's a comet! Don't expect me to talk about him again. Our relationship is a secret. You're the only person I'm telling," Judith says, "And don't worry about me."

Judith knows that given half a chance Eva will explain every reason why she should worry about her, drag all Judith's mistakes out onto the table like dead cats, so to get her off track, Judith asks about Alan Michael, and lets Eva talk until the kitchen is filled with drifts of soft gray wings, heaps of dead moth words. And sometimes Judith retreats, imagining Jean-Claude's delights.

And then after a hurried dinner, the Blumenthals are going. Alan Michael deigns to give his honorary Aunt a peck on the cheek, the Walkman still going *chkkk chkkkk chkkkk*, and apologizes again about the fried microwave, and Leonard, who Judith knows is itching to get into the car and turn on the radio, squeezes her shoulders, and Eva hugs her longer than usual, happy to be taking home the secret of Jean-Claude, though she wouldn't trade her Leonard for any man.

Finally, Judith is alone again, and all the radios and the television are off.

"Thank you, Jean-Claude," Judith says to her creation. "If you were here right now I'd lave your feet from pure gratitude." She laughs at her words and at the image of washing his feet; she laughs at how the cleanser inspired his coming into her life like a comet; she laughs at how the date on the calendar had given him his age, the actor his name. She laughs when she asks herself if Jean-Claude is more a product of her imagination than what she sees in the men she really dates, than what Eva sees in her Leonard Dear.

She looks around her kitchen, the gap on the counter where the new microwave will go. "Tomorrow," she says.

She heads for her study to put words on paper, blamelessly inventing truth, and, as the image of Jean-Claude as a heavenly body dims, she settles into the silent twilight.

BEAUTY CANNOT KEEP

When the doorbell rings, Rachel drains her glass of vodka, tugs at her cuffs, and reminds herself that this time will be different. She rakes her fingers through her graying auburn hair and opens the door to welcome three old friends, and, on Joel's arm, the latest in his string of young women.

The four friends stand laughing and hugging in the narrow vestibule. When Richard envelops Rachel in a bear hug, she feels the chill of the late winter night on his overcoat. And then it is Karin's turn. "So glad you're home again," Karin whispers.

Almost before the two women have stepped back, Joel swoops over. During the tumult of the greetings, Jenny remains in the hall but soon stands by Joel's side, her small hand in his.

Rachel's lost count of the young women Joel brought to meet her—for her to compare to herself at their age, when she'd gone about on his arm as "Joel's girl." They're always in their early twenties, as though he'd discovered the best age for a woman and stuck with it.

She welcomes Jenny as she welcomed all the others—with a sort of genial neutrality, knowing, as they did not, of their temporary place in Joel's life and therefore hers. Jennifer drops Joel's hand as she is introduced to Rachel, and Rachel notices annoyance flicker over Joel's face as though his little prize had been taken from him. Her hand was soon nestled back in his.

Rachel looks at Joel's newest girl: part child, Alice-in-Wonderland face, lank blond hair falling straight to the shoulders. The level way she returns Rachel's gaze of frank appraisal suggests that she's of a different mettle than the others. Rachel wants to take the girl's chin in her hand and turn her face to the light, and she feels her own face flush. Listening to Joel's proud catalogue of Jenny's education, travels and accomplishments, she realizes that Jenny must be older than she had thought. And what should it matter tonight?

They all sit around the coffee table with drinks in hand and cheese and crackers on the table. Jenny sits on the floor, her head resting against Joel's knees with what he calls "the flexibility of youth." Whatever had she seen in him? Still, his limitations are no worse than others'—only more evident. The conversation was part the familiar talk common to people in their set who'd known one another for years, part gossip, part disbelief about the corrupt state of politics, art, and academe.

Bright red tulips flare in a blue and white pitcher. In the hospital Rachel wanted to reread Plath, but the hospital bookmobile and library had no Plath. Nor Sexton. Bad examples. The rooms up and down the corridor were filled with bad examples.

Jenny's bright mouth is fixed in a sociable smile. "Is this chatter boring you?" Rachel asks.

"Thanks to Joel I feel like I know everyone you're talking about."

Rachel knows a social lie when she hears one, and when Richard asks about Steve, she tells Jenny it's her brother.

"She knows who Steve is," Joel interposes, an edge in his tone

Jenny's smile of gratitude contradicts him. For a moment nobody speaks, and then Karin breaks the awkward silence. She reaches down and picks up the paperback on the end table. "I've been meaning to read this. It got such mixed reviews. Have you finished it?"

"It's ok. It's right in the tradition of 'the woman always gets it in the end'—throws herself under a train, takes poison, drowns. "

"The reviews said she was killed but didn't say how."

"The writing's not bad. Take it with you. I won't want to read it again."

"High praise from someone who rarely parts with a book," said Joel.

"No, it's just not something I want to read again. You might like it, Karin. And pass it along when you're done—or keep it."

"Thanks," she says, replacing the book. "Have you been writing?"

"Some mirrors I don't want to look into right now."

"You're too good..." Richard says.

Karin says that the jade plant is doing well. "It reminded me of you, somehow, and so I sent it."

"It seems to survive no matter what. The more I abuse it, the happier it seems to be."

"Like some women need more abuse than others," Jenny says. How like one of Joel's pronouncements! Confident and heedless of the effect it might have.

"Joel said you were in India last summer. I used to think that I didn't want to die until I'd been to Marabar. You know that part of *Passage to India* when they're in the cave and the echo goes round and round like a great coiling worm?" She pauses, telling herself she's babbling.

"Used to? What made you change your mind?" Jenny asked.

Rachel shrugs. She asks, "Where did you go?"

"The usual tourist stuff, the Taj and temples. The caves aren't really in Marabar. There's Barabar, and caves that are supposed to echo in Nagarjunya... It was mostly the caves I'd wanted to see. Or hear? It was a kind of pilgrimage."

"And?" prompts Karin.

"It was almost dead inside." She looks down at her fingernails. Not until then does Rachel notice how short they are. Then Jenny looks up to meet Rachel's gaze. "So maybe you'd better not go. Just hold on to your ideas of Marabar..."

"Which really isn't Marabar at all..."

"And why should the caves be different?" Joel says.

"Or this night?" Rachel adds.

When they're at the table for dinner, Rachel asks Richard to fill the glass at the empty chair. "He'll be getting here after you've all gone. I thought I'd set the place for him now anyway. And fill his glass."

"Are you sure pouring fresh wouldn't taste better?" Joel asks.

"Oh, probably. But it's a little tradition we have. It makes him feel expected."

"And who is this he? What's his name?" asks Richard. "Is he special?"

"Have you known him long?" Karin is never shy about her questions. "When will we meet him?"

"In time. You'll meet him, I assure you. I'd rather not tell you his name just yet, but yes, he's special."

"You're in love?" asks Joel, teasing, a note of incredulity in his voice. "And you didn't tell us?"

"I'm telling you now. Half in love."

"'Half in love with easeful Death,'" murmurs Jenny. "Keats."

He hasn't told her, and she's picked up Joel's habit of hearing half a quotation, finishing it and identifying it by author.

The dinner-table talk is what Rachel calls the Sunday *Times* in review.

While Karin's taking the coffee into the living room, Rachel tidies up the kitchen. She accepts Jenny's offer to help, in spite of preferring to be alone. The women Joel brought by seemed to think that occupying Joel's bed conferred rights to be in her kitchen.

Jenny leans against the counter as Rachel bends into the refrigerator. "Sometimes he doesn't have a clue," she says.

Surprised, Rachel straightens and turns to face her. How had he hurt Jenny?

Once he'd poured her shot after shot of vodka directly from the freezer. She'd been surprised at its slightly sweet taste. Finally the air itself had seemed warm and syrupy.

74

"I've got to lie down, she'd said, "I don't feel so well." He was solicitous, apologetic for her queasiness, and offered her the privacy of his bedroom. Closing the door behind her, she'd peeled off her clothes, turned out the light, and stretched out on his bed. When she awoke feeling woozy, she wasn't alone.

The drawer next to the bed opened and closed, and he was on top of her. She must have passed out again because he was lying by her side insisting that she tell him she had loved it. Through waves of nausea and disbelief she finally told the only acceptable lie.

"You don't have to say anything," Jenny says. "He's your friend, after all."

"And your boyfriend."

"But what I mean is, he shouldn't have brought me here. Not tonight."

"Oh, you know you're..."

"Being welcome has nothing to do with it. It has nothing to do with you, or..."

"Or everything?"

"I am glad I came, though." Jenny brushes a wisp of hair from her face. Her voice is breathy. "I read your books. Joel showed me the ones you'd given him. I read them all a couple of times."

"Oh?"

"I didn't want to say anything with the others listening. They're a mirror for for me, too. I wanted you to know. It's important that you know." Her voice trembles though it's not much louder than a whisper.

Rachel looks down into Jenny's small face. "A mirror..." She thinks that if she were to bend closer she could see her reflection in the wide unblinking eyes whose gaze met her own. "And what do you see?"

Before Jen could speak, Richard calls, "Need any help?"

"We're fine. We'll be out in a minute," Jenny says resting her hand on Rachel's wrist. This is her answer. And Rachel places her other hand on Jen's wrist, almost as though she means to take her pulse. Is this the same woman who'd curled up at Joel's feet?

As they were getting ready to leave, Jenny gestures towards the dinner table where the solitary place setting with its full glass of deep red wine. She frowns and asks, "Are you sure he'll be here?"

"Late. You'll all be home snug as bugs."

At the door, Richard bends close to Rachel to whisper to her, "Take care." And Karin hugs her, matching his affection. Joel squeezes Rachel's hand, and leads the now docile Jenny away.

Rachel stands in her doorway, while they walk down the long narrow apartment hallway to the elevator. Jenny tugs herself free of Joel and runs towards her, and Rachel steps back into her apartment.

Jenny touches Rachel's face, the flat of her palm on her cheek. She tilts her small pale face up towards Rachel's. Rachel is surprised at how soft her lips are, at how they yield beneath hers, yet promise nothing. "Remember," Jenny says and is gone before Rachel can manage a reply.

She wants to call after her, to tell her something, anything that will protect her.

She leans against the closed door of her apartment for a moment, then walks back to the living room. Other women would have filled such a sunny room with a tangle of plants, watering, spraying and pinching. They would have found joy in their contained forest of Boston ferns and spider plants, dieffenbachia, ficus, philodendron, and annually gaudy Christmas cactus. Other women would have bathed and polished the leaves of their rubber trees, cut and re-rooted corn plants. They would have watched their souvenir remnants of romantic dinner parties, toothpick-spitted avocado pits, sprout into spindly plants and grow before meting out a casual death after a lover's quarrel.

The bare window, empty of plants, holds her reflection like a mirror. She says aloud, "'Where Beauty cannot keep her lustrous eyes, Or new Love pine at them beyond tomorrow.' Keats." The place setting and goblet of wine remain.

She returns to the apartment door and, as if at a signal, she opens it wide. "Everything's ready."

She closes the door and walks to the table, lifting the goblet and holding it between her and the lamp so that she could enjoy the ruby glint. She lifts it as a toast to her last guest. "'O, for a draft of vintage,'" she begins and drains the glass, "'that hath been cool'd a long age in the deep-delved earth,'"

She carries the goblet and the rest of the place setting to the kitchen, where she puts them in the dishwasher, which she switches on. She will be tidy this time.

She fills a glass with vodka from the freezer, adding no ice. "'That I might drink, and leave the world unseen...'" Walking down the hall to the bathroom, she continues her recitation, "'Where but to think is to be full of sorrow And leaden-eyed despair...'"

She turns as if to beckon someone forward. She sets the glass of vodka on the sink and opens the medicine chest, takes out bottles of pills and capsules, and empties them into her hand: yellow, red, pale blue, green and white. She looks down into her palm, her hand so full, that as she trembles slightly, three pills fall into the sink and roll down the drain.

She recites, "'Darkling I listen; and for many a time I have been half in love with easeful Death, Call'd him soft names in many a mused rhyme, To take into the air my quiet breath...'" Her hand grows cold holding the vodka glass, "'Now more than ever seems it rich to die, To cease upon the midnight with no pain,...'"

She sets the glass back down.

Hoarded pills fill her upturned palm—Valium, Dalmane,

Halcyon, Ativan, Seconal, and Prozac. She looks at the pills and sees her pale wrist mapped with scars. She covers these scars with her right hand, and as she does so, she remembers a wrist as yet unmarked.

She takes a deep breath. Then she spills the pills into the green plastic cup in the toothbrush holder. They clatter as they fall and bounce in the cup. She shuts the cabinet with a firm click. The glass of vodka she drains. Looking in the mirror, she speaks as if at someone beside her. "Not tonight," she says to whoever's listening. "Not this story. Not this time."

At The Set Time

Ishould have been worried when I noticed that he smelled like freshly washed sheets, line dried in the summer sun. Or when I examined his image, reflected with mine in the window glass, deciding that he looked enough like me to be my son.

The laboratory where I work as a research chemist hires a few college students as vacation replacements. The worst are a combination of smarminess and arrogance. Early on, I concluded that Dave was neither. He was charming: leaning over the table at lunch as though all the rest of the world had ceased to exist, he asked just the right questions about the direction of our research. His face gave away his every emotion.

One Monday morning soon after he'd begun work, he came in early, smiling. He'd spent Sunday in the library and found an article in the latest issue of *Nature* that he thought might have an application to our work; he'd brought me a photocopy of it. After listening to what he had to say, I agreed that he just might be right. He'd brought a sheaf of papers, data that he'd analyzed. I was impressed.

Once, leaning against the centrifuge, he said with no context, "It's amazing how much baggage people carry with them."

The glassware and metal of the lab gleamed. The gray work surfaces shone in the light. I wondered what he would say about baggage when he reached my age.

Then late in July he came to work looking different. Instead of his conventional Oxford cloth shirts, that day he wore a silk shirt, the color of sweet butter. He had his sleeves rolled up. He was tall, with the kind of body only a young man who doesn't work out can have. The shirt said, "Touch me."

Around four o'clock, he looked at me over his beaker of

coffee and murmured that he was "running on empty."

He said, "It's funny how you can go all day on no sleep and feel great."

He told me that he'd had a date the night before that began on the steps of the Art Museum.

I imagined them sitting on the steps looking down the wide tree-lined Parkway leading to the city lights. The spotlit fountains marked intervals leading up to the LOVE sculpture with its nearby pillar of water. But I said nothing and the subject dropped.

He hadn't mentioned a woman since he'd told me about Lisa the first night he came to my apartment for dinner. He'd lived with Lisa for more than a year, and he was trying to figure out what he wanted months after she'd moved out

"I don't want to go back with her unless we can make it work." He used his fork to pick a choice morsel from the chicken on the serving platter.

"What do your friends say?"

"They think she's wonderful. After all, she's smart, and beautiful, and charming."

I didn't want to hear any more about her virtues. "So?"

"They don't know that she's made my life a living hell." He paused, then continued, "As crazy as she is, I really do love her."

I'd been married, knew about love and living hell. I wasn't about to tell him any part of it.

From then on whenever I went out with my friends, I scouted the room when we walked in, half-expecting to see Dave leaning over a table, his fingers woven into a lover's clasp.

Somehow our dinner on Friday became a habit. Then one night after what had become our routine kitchen cleanup we sat together in the study at opposite ends of the sofa, our arms stretched out across the top of the sofa's back. He stroked my hand. "You don't have to be careful, Sarah. I won't leave you."

Tears came to my eyes. I turned away a moment, hoping he

wouldn't notice, being careful.

He invited me to his apartment, the third floor of a Victorian house in University City. Walking up the stairs with him, passing his neighbor, who gave us a barely curious nod, for the first time in weeks I felt self-conscious with Dave.

The middle room was the bedroom. A queen-sized mattress took up most of the floor. The bed, with its white sheets, was unmade: two pillows, the sheet left in waves flung to one side. One pillow still bore the indentation of his sleeping head. I stepped back into the hall.

His bookshelves were jammed with the eclectic reading of an undergraduate. When I commented, he said he'd done a lot of reading during the years he'd been out of school. "I took six years off..."

His voice rose as though asking a question. He looked puzzled at my laughter.

"I thought you were twenty-one.

"I didn't mean to hide anything from you...Sometimes people look at you funny if they think of you as a dropout. Would it have made any difference to you?"

I shook my head no. "It's just that you seemed so..." I searched for the right word. "Precocious."

At the time I didn't think about the contradiction. In fact, he had intended to conceal something from me. I'd been feeling ridiculous, caring for him. When I learned his age, I wondered whether this embodiment of virtue, industry, honesty, and intelligence would have seemed quite so special had I recognized that his maturity was no more than I would have expected in a man his age.

When I was twenty-seven, I was working full time, had finished my PhD, and had been married for two years. His age did make a difference. He was no longer a child: this was a grown man I cared for.

On the last Friday of the summer, after we'd been talking for hours, he said, "I'm really determined to work things out with Lisa." He hadn't mentioned her name for a long time. "If we can be happy together, I want to stay with her." His voice trailed.

"You'll marry her?" I was careful to keep my question neutral.

"It's not too much to ask—to think that you have a pretty good chance of being happy, is it?"

"Is there a deadline?" I couldn't bring myself to ask directly, "Is she pregnant?"

"No deadline, but she said that she'd move to Colorado if I don't marry her."

"I know a couple of men who got married like that. They're happy—as far as I know."

"She thinks it's odd that you and I spend so much time together. I told her that there's nothing to be jealous of."

Nothing. I had been dismissed.

But then he said, "My friendship with you isn't negotiable."

I remembered his having told me, "I won't leave you." I wanted to believe him. I said, "It might have to be negotiable. But I hope you'd explain to me so that you wouldn't just disappear."

When the summer was over, we kept in touch sporadically by phone. I imagined conversations with him, talking to him as though talking to a younger, better part of myself. When he called in mid-October, I invited him to dinner, and he agreed.

He arrived harried. "I was at the hospital with Lisa last night."

"What happened? Is she all right?" I repeated the question, imagining the worst. He had lied to me. There had been a pregnancy. Every story I had ever heard of a botched abortion replayed itself. "Is she all right?"

I was surprised at my need for reassurance. After all, who was this girl to me: she who had made his life a living hell, who set his eyes alight with pleasure.

"She's all right. She's pregnant. There was some fluid."

"When is she due?"

"This week."

Somehow I managed to produce a semblance of sincere congratulations. What would he have said in August if, instead of asking him about having a deadline, I had asked him if Lisa was pregnant.

"Do me a favor," he said. "Call her."

"You want me to call her?" I struggled to keep outrage and incredulity from my voice.

"I want you to be a part of my life—and if it's going to work, she has to want you to be a part of her life, too."

I told him I would, but that I couldn't promise that I'd do it right away. I couldn't imagine the conversation I would have with her. And then I realized that he didn't know how much he was asking of me. I had been careful, so careful that apparently he hadn't the slightest idea of how I felt about him.

"I said I'd be here tonight—and I am, but I have to get back to Lisa in case her water breaks. I have her car." He looked at his watch. "I have to go. I promised her I'd only stay a half-hour."

I thought, How could you leave her? Why are you here? I kept silent.

He answered my unspoken questions, all of them, with "I promised to be here tonight." And then he was gone.

A few minutes after he left, the phone rang. I didn't answer.

And then for days I didn't hear anything more. I rethought what he'd said during the summer. His remark about "baggage" was no longer amusing. Though young, he had as much baggage with this pregnancy as I had with my own much-regretted childlessness.

When Lisa said she'd move to Colorado, it was no ordinary ploy to get him to make a commitment; it was a threat to move away with his child. His life must have been a hell, far more than I had ever imagined. He'd only alluded to what was happening to him, to what he'd been feeling. Just as he had no sense of how I'd come to love him, I'd guessed nothing of what he'd been suffering.

Still no word.

What could I have expected? Who was I, really, that he might call me from the hospital to say that Lisa had gone into labor; to say that all had gone well and that he was a father? And if he had called, how would I have felt hearing him say that another woman had given birth to his child? Even if he had come to love me, whatever else I could have offered him, what I wanted most to give, wanted most to have, was impossible. I would never have been able to have his child: I was, simply, too old.

On Friday when I was putting together papers to take some work home, I heard a tap on the open door. Dave leaned against the doorframe, looking drunk with exhaustion and exhilaration. "It's a boy. Lisa picked the name. 'Isaac.' Do you like it?"

"It's a fine name." I laughed. He was wholly unaware of the irony of her choice. "A fine name. I couldn't have chosen a better one myself." I didn't explain the biblical reference.

"We've been up for 72 hours, but I wanted to stop by on my way home to tell you the news in person."

I gestured towards a silver heart on his jacket. "I haven't seen that before."

"It's from the baby heart monitor that they put on Lisa's belly. She stuck it on me before I left the hospital." I leaned forward to se if I could glimpse my reflection in its surface. All I could see were amorphous shapes and colors. He must have been too far away, and I could find nothing of myself in his shining heart.

NEIGHBOR

If she heard "At War with Satan" one more time, Kathleen told herself, she'd have to go to confession. Through the thin walls that separated her row house from the Delahantys' she listened to the battle of the generations playing itself out in music. Her friend Nancy blasted oldies, but Nancy's teenage son, Sean, and his satanic rock were winning the skirmish, if not the war. Kathleen tried to concentrate on her talk radio program, but her mind wandered to what she heard at night through the wall, as she lay restless, waiting for sleep.

A knock at the back door brought her back to the reality of her kitchen. His long red hair bright in July sun, Sean stood on her back door stoop. The voice on the radio urged her "to go take on the day," and the news came on as Kathleen hauled herself from the vinyl chair, her thighs sticking to the seat below her shorts, prickling as she stood. "No news," she said to herself, as she switched off the radio," is good news."

Kathleen watched Sean put his face up to the door, and peer into the square of glass between the avocado valance and cafe curtain and forced a smile to her pale lips. She felt naked and ugly and old without her lipstick, without the eyebrow pencil that she used to draw pale brown brows over her hazel eyes.

Sean, shirtless and barefoot, wearing only cutoff jeans, brought the smell of stale smoke into her kitchen. It hung in his hair. Kathleen had smelled enough marijuana in her youth to recognize it. How could Nancy, who was so particular and kept her nails painted a sweet frosted pink, have raised a son like Sean? His wild curly hair rippled past his shoulders, and a tattooed snake curled down his arm onto his hand. And his piercings—they fairly sprouted like mushrooms after a rain.

Whatever would his poor father have said if he could see his son now, just the age he'd been when he'd gone to war?

"Aunt Kaydee," he said, "I need a ride." His voice had changed, but Kathleen heard the voice of the little boy just learning to talk, tugging at her skirt when the Jack and Jill ice-cream truck piped its way through the neighborhood. She'd none of her own to buy for, she had told Nancy, which Nancy knew well enough. And the vegetable dye tattoos that washed off, she'd bought him those, too, and how she and Nancy had laughed as he'd covered his arms with cartoons. Now here he stood inches taller than his father who'd come home from Nam with a flag to cover him.

They'd cried together, the two women, friends and neighbors. Nancy had showed her the medals, and Kathleen had touched the velvet of the box, and stroked the ridged silk of the ribbon and the cold embossed bronze. She'd been like a blind woman touching a face for the last time.

Kathleen stared at Sean's green eyes: over the bridge of his nose, between his eyes, a bar with steel balls. She'd learned not to ask if a piercing hurt. "Something new?"

"Yeah." He shifted his weight from one bare foot to the other. "So can you give me a lift? Please. Mom's using the car today."

Kathleen noticed the red tongue of the snake just at the joint of his thumb. The green and black body wound its way up and around his muscled arm, the rattle ending just below his shoulder. Well, his mother had said he'd been lifting weights in the basement.

She told him that it depended on where he wanted to go and when. She had laundry to do. And he said to the El stop at Kensington and Allegheny so he could take the train into Center City to get tickets for a concert. And she'd asked whether the buses were running, knowing full well that they were, and wondered what he'd wear, but after all she wasn't his mother, and a good thing she wasn't. She kept to herself the memory of how when he got his first piercing after his ears, he and his girlfriend had both pierced their tongues. When she'd asked why, he'd actually blushed. And then she blushed too, thinking of him like that. At least she could pick up a few things at the Acme supermarket when she dropped him off.

"Did you say something, Aunt Kaydee?"

She told him that she must have been talking to herself and that she'd run him to the El in fifteen minutes after she had time to get herself together.

The snake's red tongue seemed to flicker. And then the green and black body of the snake writhed as Sean jammed his hands into the back pockets of his jeans with the casual disregard of the young for the feelings of their elders.

Her mother had warned her that impure thoughts could be read like banner headlines. She had warned her that impure thoughts led to impure deeds. She had warned her, as had the Sisters at Little Flower, even before she had entertained an impure thought, that her body was the Temple of the Holy Ghost and must not be defiled. She had been warned against occasions of sin.

And now, in her dead mother's kitchen she was endangering her soul just as she did each night that she lay alone in her narrow girlhood bed, her ear close to the wall, listening for Sean, his music, his sounds as he moved in his bed, only inches from hers just on the other side of the wall. Some nights she almost held her breath waiting, listening.

"'Without the Holy Grail,'" she murmured, "'only evil can prevail.'"

He grinned at her, his father's cocky, crooked smile. "Cool. How do you know Venom?"

Her eyes moved over his body, savoring after a long hunger. The sunlight gleamed on the ring in his nipple, caught in the few curling red gold hairs that circled the pinky brown aureoles on his flat chest, and the sunlight flared the strands on his breast bone and the line of hair that began at his navel and ran down under the waistband of his jeans.

Her lover, her Kevin, had never grown old. She liked to think of him as her Kevin, and no harm in that now, was there? Not now, not after so much time. And she'd been faithful to his memory, more faithful than many proper widows. And after all, who had been hurt, really? Her Kevin, his textures, the contrasts of silky young skin, the soft male hair, the coarse male hair. She wondered at the unyielding steel of Sean's piercings. She wanted to thread her tongue through his nipple ring and to catch hold of it in her teeth. She imagined his taste, and then his tasting her secret place, giving her pleasure as no one ever had, not even Kevin.

She had gone early to the wake. She'd sat by herself right behind Nancy to stare at Kevin's flag-covered casket. The line of friends shook hands with Nancy, hugged Nancy. Such a good friend she was, Nancy told her. Such a good friend to cry with her again and again, to cry so many bitter tears. Kathleen felt her face grow swollen with sorrow. She looked at Sean and saw his father's green, green eyes, "Holy Mother of God," she murmured. As Sean stared at her, slowly, deliberately she moved her right hand. For the first time in years she made the sign of the cross.

Devotional

1. Midnight

Just as I am falling asleep the phone rings. I do not turn on the light, but lean over and lift the receiver.

The calls no longer frighten me. No one I love is dying. Or, everyone I love is dying, and so am I. But that is not why he is calling.

Once in the morning I found the receiver next to my head on the pillow.

He speaks to me in a low voice. He asks questions I cannot remember any more than I can remember my answers. And would I tell you? What good would it do you to know what he asks of me? Would you understand why I wake with glazed thighs?

But you are curious. I can tell you are thinking of questions to ask me. I see your eyes half closed like a cat's in the sun. Your relentless questions thumb me until I am sore.

2. Beginner

Cara pulled her car into the spot next to the shiny black Mercedes sedan. She does not remember his face, and she wonders if she ever dared look him in the eye. On that day he wore an overcoat and carried a large dark gym bag.

She unlocked her car door as he approached. She repeated to herself like a mantra, "Stay in public...stay in public...stay in public." She'd told herself that the diner parking lot was public enough, but when he got into the car beside her, she wished she'd insisted on meeting him inside.

She clutched the steering wheel with both hands. The car key was in her pocket, her purse on the floor near her door. Richard, he'd said his name was, held the gym bag in his lap.

"I thought you'd like to see these," he said. He told Cara she would have to pay close attention. He reached into the bag. He pulled things out one by one and told her how they would use them. He spoke slowly. His voice was velvet and Velcro.

She remembers seeing on that first afternoon: leather restraints, a dildo, condoms for the dildo, latex gloves, a leather mask, a funnel with a hose at its end, and a new bright red ball gag.

He explained to her again about the safe word. She wondered aloud how she would use a safe word with the ball gag in her mouth. He did not answer. He told her she must choose a safe word.

She chose "devotional."

3. Hot Wax

A candle flickers on a shelf above the counter in the dimly lit room. A pot sits on a one-burner hot plate. The room smells like honey. Wearing a short white terry-cloth sarong, I stand barefoot next to the bed. I am waiting for Desirée.

She opens the door just wide enough to slip through and glances at a slip of paper she holds in her hand. I lie on the table and watch as she plunges a flat piece of wood through the crust on the hot wax in the pot and stirs. I have listened to Desirée as her marriage fell to pieces, and her revenge for having received my sympathy continues to play itself out in this small room.

"Half-leg wax, bikini wax," she says, "you go away with boyfriend for weekend?"

Before I must answer she continues, "Next time you get

Brazilian wax." Desirée smiles knowingly, "men love Brazilian."

"Like doctor," she said the first time that I opened my legs wide so she could spread the hot wax. She leaned forward, adding, "I see so much... I see nothing."

As she tucks tissues into the crotch of my panties she tells me that one of her clients came in and told her to take all her hair off. Desirée says, "Her husband want it like little girl." She pauses. "What you think of that?" Her voice is soft.

She pulls the leg elastic up and inward, and has me hold the cloth in place while she paints my bikini line and pubis with hot wax. When the wax hardens, she pulls it off, ripping out my hair by its roots.

She does this more than once. Each time the soothing warmth of the wax, then a flash of pain, sharp as thousands of hot needles. I have come to anticipate the pain. It fades slowly. Desirée powders me with talc as though I am a baby.

"You perfect now. Smooth. You go away with boyfriend for weekend." Desirée does not ask me now.

"Thank you." I say to her, for tonight I will talk with you. I will tell you all of this: How, coated with hot wax, I think of you as the heat enters my body. How I lie perfectly still waiting for the pain. Tonight on the telephone I will offer you my pain, my devotional.

4. Don't

The last thing Cara remembered saying was, "Don't." But because it was not her safe word, the people who stood over her did not stop. They continued using her until each one had finished, and by that time Cara had lost consciousness.

Nothing like that is supposed to happen, of course.

Using the safe word is part of the ritual, but Cara's master, D., should have been looking after her. In fact, he was looking after her, and in his judgment he was providing her with an experience of sublime surrender, yielding to his will, and through him to his friends. Her submission to them was another form of her service to him. And when they were satisfied, they left him alone with her. It was a matter of respect that was his due.

Mistakes will happen. To be sure, this scene was a mistake.

Even when Cara lay silent, limp, her master was not alarmed. He took a certain pride in his training. That Cara had endured rather than using her safe word, he saw as a tribute to himself. If Cara had known him in other circumstances, she would, perhaps, have realized that his personality was not suited to assuming responsibility for another's well-being, for another's pleasure. He was too selfish, too arrogantly self-absorbed to pay the necessary close attention to his slave.

And he did not appreciate Cara.

She came to him already trained, through Stephen, who was a friend of Alan, who was a friend of Marta, who was a friend of Richard, who had first fastened the collar on Cara's neck. She had passed through their hands, being prepared, made ready for the next person she would serve.

She lay, her hands bound behind her back, naked except for the black leather restraints on her wrists and ankles, and, of course, the collar.

Her dark hair stuck to her body, wet with perspiration, tears, semen and saliva. D. stood over her. He prodded her abdomen with his boot. And then again harder. He would not have called it a kick. And again, an expression of distaste distorting his features. Cara lay on her back, her head tilted, her mouth slightly open. Her lips were pale now, a spot of dried blood where her lip was split.

D. took an ice cube in his hand and glided it over her nipples, which rose, puckering, as he made slow circles. Even unconscious she could serve his desire. Her eyelids fluttered open. He came slowly into focus, and she spoke only one word, "Devotional."

5. The Collar

Cara walked down the set of steps and opened the door. Her pocket was stuffed with cash. She'd done her homework and looked online, leaving, she knew, an electronic trail, but as with breadcrumbs she'd been unable to retrace her steps, to return home. Or perhaps she'd returned home changed by what she'd seen. Still, she didn't want to use her charge card or a check here. Paying in cash meant shame. Shame was good. She wore it like a collar.

These days she dressed without looking in the mirror. No one else knew all the secrets she knew, and she could not meet her own eyes. In the world she laughed, answered the phone easily, bought a skinny latte grande at Starbucks and joked with the barista. In the world she was safe, had the illusion of being safe. Rarely did she meet someone who looked at her in the singular way she had come to recognize.

Only at home was she enslaved. Daily. And that is what brought her here. She had not been to a party in months. Ever since D. had left, the door shuddering when it slammed behind him, she had been without a Master. She did not seek a replacement for him any more than she had sought him. He had merely appeared as the others had appeared only when she was prepared for them and for her service. None had been as exacting as her Mistress.

No jangling bell announced her presence in the store. Here she was surrounded by the things she had seen for the first time in Richard's car and later come to know: ball gags, dildos, leather, masks, the softest leather restraints, and collars. Richard had been her first teacher. After him there had been others. Each had been increasingly strict, more able to subdue her rebellion. The latest, most strict was D.. When D. left, he took the collar with him. "You are not worthy to wear it," he seethed, removing it from her bent neck as she stood before him, sobbing. Later she would not know if her grief was for him or for her lost service.

She hated living without a proper Master. But she refused to answer ads. When the calls came inviting her to parties, the first few times she explained that D. had gone. And then the calls stopped. She wondered who D. had sitting on the floor at his feet now. It didn't matter. It only mattered that for some unbearable weeks she had wandered free, like a feral cat aching to be tamed. And so she yielded to the Mistress who now ruled her from the moment she entered what should have been her sanctuary until the time she escaped into the street and safety.

It was to serve her that she was buying the collar. With the modest gestures to which she had become accustomed, she pointed to the collar in the case. The sales girl suggested a day-glow plastic dildo, which she swore was almost indistinguishable from the real thing. She took the neon green object from the case and held it up, bent it, held it out. "Touch it," she said, Cara obeyed. "Basic. No motor. Natural, huh?" Cara had others, better, she thought, at home, but she fished into her pocket and pulled out more bills. The sales girl flashed a conspiratorial smile, and gave her both the collar and a new dildo still in its plastic case.

At home she washed the dildo with soap and water, held it up to the light. It was the color of a pitcher of lime Kool Aid in the sun. She tossed it onto the bed. It made a soft thud as it landed.

Cara showered, prepared herself as she'd been taught for an evening of service. It was no less than her Mistress required, but without the collar she had been unable to serve her properly. Now all was ready. Wearing a bath towel like a sarong, Cara stood in front of the mirror. Now her gaze met her own. She fastened the collar around her neck, which was still damp from the shower. That was a mistake. The collar would certainly chafe. But it was too late.

She stared at herself. The new collar was stiff, but she wore it as though she had always been encircled by its safety. The D rings gleamed in the lamplight. Cara hooked her thumbs into the towel, and with a single simple gesture she stood naked in front of the mirror. She stared into the mirror, wondering at her daring. "I am here to serve you, Mistress," she said.

She would not need the lubricant. Within minutes her cries of passion filled the room. After nearly an hour of increasingly intense spasms, limbs flailing, she murmured her safe word and lay at last still. Had you been there you would have heard as I did, "Devotional."

DROWNING

It is the evening of the third day, and the fluorescent light is flickering. Will tells himself that if the flicker is related to the headache making a tight fist behind his right eye, the light will be steady tomorrow. If he's here. He's never been comfortable in hospital waiting rooms, in spite of the efforts of gray ladies holding out offers of scorched coffee in Styrofoam cups. The magazines, *Time, People, America*, and *St. Anthony Messenger,* greasy with being thumbed by strangers, are outdated. No one looking at these magazines can read any news they might care about. That news will come in green from around corners, down corridors, behind swinging doors. The headache's fist rotates.

Will drops the copy of *Time* back onto the heap of magazines. Across the room a woman brushes her lank brown hair from her face. The woman, who seems about his age, looks familiar, but as he nears fifty, almost all women remind him of someone else: this one's brow, that one's hair, another's mouth or chin. Bodies are like or unlike those he has known and dismissed. Will looks for a wedding band.

He wishes he could be waiting for news of his father with a wife, if not here by his side in Ottumwa, then expecting his call at home in Philadelphia caring for their cereal-box children. Instead his neighbor James will come and feed the cats. "Who'll wait like this for me?" he wonders. "Maybe it's just as well, if I have my father's luck with wives."

Will feels a stab of disloyalty to his dead mother, but not to the woman his father married after his mother died. What would she say—or feel—if she learned that his father was, perhaps, dying?

He's fourteen, standing on the farmhouse porch with his

father, the light over the door burning into the Iowa winter night. They've come back to find the door locked, two suitcases on the porch. The smaller suitcase is strapped shut with his belts. They ring the bell and Will pounds on the door. He looks into the parlor window. The lights are on, but the room is empty. He can break the glass window of the door and turn the latch. They can get in if they want to. He can smash the red china vase on the piano, pull down the green velvet drapes, take the photograph he hates from the mantle and stomp hard so glass slashes the picture of the six Susskind children and their parents. The parlor has no framed photograph of him and his father with the woman and her children. He would rip it up, throw it on the coals of the stove and watch the pieces curl to ash. His father's hand is light on his shoulder for a moment and then gone. Why isn't his father even a little angry? His father carries their suitcases to car and stands in the snowy driveway waiting for him.

The windshield wiper swishes aside the snow that the wind blows up from the fields. Does this have anything to do with staying with Grandma Wissenlicht all last week? He wants to ask, but instead blinks back angry tears. He's been a good boy. During the long drive into town his father offers no explanations, as he had offered none about Will's mother's rages, her disappearances, her medications, her death.

Will thinks of Trude Susskind Wissenlicht as "the-woman-my-father-married-after-my-mother-died," not as "my father's second wife," never "stepmother." Once, when James had referred to the woman as his "stepmother," he said, "She's not my mother. She was never my mother." James had said that whether Will liked it or not, though not his mother, a stepmother was what she was. For weeks afterwards he hadn't spoken to James about his grievances.

Every day he thinks about his mother. Her wild cries as she lay sobbing on the sofa. Her lovely, crumpled body that he found on the living room floor that last day. And every day he thinks about the woman his father married after his mother died. His hatred is a stone it takes much of his energy to carry, and he carries it with him everywhere. Even here.

A crucifix hangs crooked near the television. Crucifixes are everywhere in the hospital. Remember. He suffered. He died for you. Offer it up. Offer it up. Offer it up. Certainly his father had, seventy-eight years of it. Still, Will envies the peace he'd seen on his father's face when together they'd knelt at the rail by the altar, mouths open to receive the host. Of course he shouldn't have been looking at his father during communion, but for the last few years, his concentration has faltered. He's afraid that if he goes to straighten it, the Sister of Mercy patrolling the corridor might consider it a rebuke.

A nun calls out his name, William Wissenlicht, and he raises his hand like a seventh grader, "Here, Sister." He stands, waiting for the news, but if there were real news, he'd be seeing the doctor or a priest. She tells him the surgery has started later than expected, not to worry "more than necessary." He's grateful that she hasn't added any sanctimonious platitudes. He'll be here for hours more. He could've brought a brief with him to work on. He has to argue a case next week and his client is guilty of murder. What he does best, he thinks, is to plead the case for the guilty.

The woman with whom he's been exchanging speculative looks is standing in front of him. Yes, she's wearing a wedding band. He hauls himself to his feet again. Manners.

"Excuse me, "she says, "Did I hear Sister call you William Wissenlicht?" Will nods. "I thought you looked familiar. My mother married a William Wissenlicht, and we were on the farm together about thirty-five years ago? I was Rebecca...I mean, I am Rebecca. Rebecca Schultz now, I married Gus from the farm down the road."

Just what I need now, one of them, he thinks. "Oh,

Rebecca…," he says, "which one were you?"

"Fourth from oldest, two younger brothers. I was the girl who followed you around." She pauses. "Oh, you wouldn't remember. Anyway… " She touches his arm for a moment and her voice drops. "You're here for your dad?"

He nods.

"You look just like him. I was looking at photographs with Timothy, the baby, last week, and there you both were with the rest of us. It was our first Christmas as a family. You stood looking kind of off to the side, like you were ready to bolt."

"Is that how it seemed? Well, . . . " Where were these family photos?

"You must have missed your mother something awful, it being the first Christmas after she died."

She was right, but he didn't want to grant her so much as a nod.

"Did you know we didn't have anything left from the insurance from our father? I think Mom hoped your dad would save us or something, which I guess he tried his best to do. There wasn't much for presents.

"I'm sorry," she said, shaking her head. "I started to run on and never even asked about your dad."

For a moment Will thought she was going to put her hand on his arm. He put his hands in his pockets. "He's having a growth removed from his lung. We hope it's not malignant."

"We?"

"My father and I. Just the two of us." He managed a wan smile.

"But you live in Philadelphia now, don't you?"

"How did you know?"

"Wonders of the web. Before Mom died four years ago we looked you up, thinking to let you know what was happening to her, though why you'd want to hear when you… "

What did she want him to say? Common decency required

a denial, but before he'd formulated even a basic demurrer, she was chattering at him again.

"She never stopped talking about you, Will, wondering if you'd grown up all right. She said you were such a sensitive child. She hoped you wouldn't suffer too much along the way," Rebecca says. "She died of breast cancer. She suffered terribly herself."

"I'm sorry," Will says, the words roll out like marbles.

"Thanks. My sister Edith is being operated on today, same thing. Christ, I keep thinking I'm next. I hope my language doesn't offend you."

He shook his head, "I'm sorry to hear about all your trouble."

"Do you mind if I sit down with you?" Without waiting for an answer she sits on the chair next to the one he'd been in, and, automatically, he sits too. "I'm sure you've enough of your own. We all do. Do you have children?"

"Two cats, Merton and Jezebel. And you?"

"Three boys." Rebecca opens her purse, and Will thinks she's going to take out a wallet thick with pictures of her family, but she takes a tissue from her purse and dabs at her eyes. "You loved cats way back then too. You used to sneak out after dinner to feed the barn cats what you left on your plate.

"Golly! You and Mom had such a fight over her drowning kittens! I thought for sure you'd hurt her real bad the way she went down to the ground so sudden." Rebecca shakes her head.

"All I remember," he says, "was trying to keep her from drowning the poor helpless little things."

"She hated doing it. You didn't understand about how there'd be hundreds of cats in a year or two, and them all starving and turning wild. How could you? Some farms, why, the men would break their necks, quicker than drowning. My father used to, but then after....Your father.... Mom hadn't any choice. She let you pick one from the litter, remember? You chose a little orange one with blue eyes we called Tigger."

"Why not just take them to the shelter?"

"Nobody in Ottumwa wants shelter kittens, what with all the litters barn cats have, not to mention the house cats. I guess they could have gone to the shelter and lived a while in cages until they got gassed."

"I still think...." Did he have to hear all this now? He remembered Tigger, but not the photo. Were they living in parallel worlds?

He hadn't a chance to say what he thought before she continued.

"So Mom has to put the kittens in a tied sack with a rock in the bottom to weight it down. You can just about hear them through the burlap, kind of mewing, and the sack is all squirmy. You're trying to push her away from the barrel of water, and you can't. She drops in the sack. It sinks clear down to the bottom, and you reach way down in and haul it up. You can see them still moving inside, though not as much as before, so then Mom and you have a kind of tug of war with that bag of kittens dripping water over the both of you, and both of you crying now, both crying over drowning kittens. Each time she gets a hold of the bag she'd puts it back in the barrel and you pull it up, and each time the bag looks heavier, water just pouring out. And when she opens the bag to check that they're none of them suffering, and you pull it loose from her one last time, both of you soaking wet now, that's when she loses her balance—or you push her—I was never sure which. She always said she lost her balance. And you, you're off like a shot straight to the barn, and by the time Mom and I get over there you have all those kittens laid out in a row with the rock at the end like a headstone."

"I didn't push her," Will says, but he isn't sure that he didn't. "You know so much. Why did she lock us out?"

Rebecca sighs. "I'm not sure you want to know this."

"Believe me, I do."

"I feel funny, and your father sick. It's...."

"You know. Why shouldn't I? That is, at least you know what she told you."

"What were you told?"

Will, having been told nothing, doesn't answer.

After a moment and a deep breath she says, "OK. My bedroom and Alice's was right next to theirs so I heard stuff I know I wasn't supposed to hear. The Church was really strict about birth control, even more than now. It seemed all you had to do was look at Mom and she'd get pregnant—that's how come there were so many of us—and they'd been married maybe three months when she missed a period. He says that she'd got pregnant again on purpose, and she swears she must have miscalculated. This argument goes on night after night. Then one morning I see her carry bloody sheets from their room. So she'd just been late or maybe she had miscarried. It happens like that sometimes."

"What did that have to do with being locked out?"

"One night I heard him say he can't afford to feed more children, and that she has too many already.

"I didn't try to listen, but I didn't sleep well, and their voices would wake me up. I heard tones mostly, hers pleading, his angry. And then one night I hear him say, 'If that's the way you feel about what marriage means, I'll take Will and move out.' I heard her sobbing through the rest of the night. I don't know that he slept either. I didn't. Of course I didn't exactly understand what he meant at the time. I was too young. I just knew it was trouble. Later I realized that he wouldn't let her touch him, and he didn't want to touch her."

"But she locked us out. You can't explain that away."

"I'm not trying to make excuses. You asked me what happened," Rebecca said, a hint of chill in her voice. "Do you still want to know? I can go back across the room and we can just pretend none of this happened."

"No. Go on, really." And he meant it.

"He told her to leave your clothes on the porch. He didn't want to see any of us again. Mom made us stay upstairs in the back bedroom until you'd gone. She cried and cried. It was awful."

"It was no barrel of laughs for me, either," he said. The door is shut tight against him, and the frozen night is in him yet.

"You know, Will, the whole truth is that it I looked you up while Mom was still alive. She was real sick, and I thought you might come to see her."

"Why would I have done that?"

"That's what my brother Steven said. He said, 'Rebecca, if Will did come, he'd spit in her face. He hated her.'

"You didn't hate her that much, not really, did you?"

"Not to speak ill of the dead, but your sainted mother did, after all, say to me, and these are her exact words, 'Nothing you can ever do, will make me love you.'"

"Oh, Will, She didn't say that to you. I was there. It was right after the kittens got drowned. We're by the barn, the three of us, you and Mom both soaking wet, her clothes and arms muddy with the fall. She'd scraped her arm, and it's bleeding. She tries to put her arm around you, and you won't let her touch you. You stand with your arms out to your sides like you're guarding the dead kittens, and you won't move. She begs you to come into the house, says she'll make you sugar cookies.

"Then you say it to her, just as clear as could be, 'Nothing you can ever do will make me love you.' It nearly broke her heart. What she does say, and maybe this is what you kept with you all these years, she says, 'You are a motherless child and there isn't nothing I can do about it. Nothing. Unless you let me give you what I can of a mother's love.' She says, 'I don't want to take your mother's place. I can't do that any more than the six children I have above ground can take the place of Peter, my first and stillborn.'" Rebecca dabs at her eyes again, and shakes her head, as though rejecting something he can't see.

Looking for signs of deceit, Will studies her. She's quiet now, now, the set of her shoulders determined, but her hands are loose in her lap. She has told the truth. He asks himself, "How can this be?"

He looks past her to stare at their reflection in the plate-glass window as though he will find the appropriate response. Everything he sees reflected appears wholly unfamiliar. "I didn't...." he says.

Will looks at Rebecca like the stranger she is. He realizes that he doesn't know if his father has ever gotten a divorce, that Rebecca might be in some way legally related to him, that she and her brothers and sisters might be entitled to share in an inheritance. A moot point. They would not accept it if it were offered; his father's legacy is entirely his own.

The fluorescent light above him buzzes like swarming bees and goes dark. A woman's voice calls code blue for a man he does not know.

ICE

In a few hours Beth will leave. She sits at her bedroom window and watches a few geese trail slow V's on the pond. In the November dawn the fields unfold a muted patchwork of stubble between the pond and the distant hills. She had lain awake for a long time before slipping from bed.

"Beth?" Bob lies on his side, hugging his pillow, facing the wall.

"Yes?"

One of the geese extends his neck, the white band bright in the dim light, and he flaps his wings as though about to take off from the surface of the pond. He settles back.

"Beth, come back." He pats her side of the bed, "Please."

It would require so little of her. She leaves her window seat. The sheets are cold. She remembers her surprise the first time he held her full length in an embrace. Never before had she been held without feeling a need to be on guard. Until then, she hadn't realized how alert she'd been in the arms of other men, how imperative their touch had been. His required no answer, has never elicited an urgent response. Still, she says, "I can't," knowing that the truth is more, "I won't." Aloud she adds, "It wouldn't do any good."

His face changed, like the surface of the pond darkened by a wind, by the shadow of a cloud.

"I'm sorry. I shouldn't have gotten back into bed," she said.

Careful not to meet his eyes, she gathers her clothes and carries them into the bathroom. She pulls the door half shut.

"You don't have to do that."

She speaks to him from behind the half-closed door. "I know I don't have to. I just am."

When she comes back in the room, he's staring at the ceiling. She pauses for a moment to look at him, but neither speaks.

"I don't understand," Bob had said again and again when she'd told him she was leaving. He'd taken her by the arms, gripping her so hard that bruises appeared in a pattern like paw prints in snow. When he saw them a few days later he was remorseful.

"They're nothing," she said of the bruises, meaning it. "They'll fade."

He had stared at her, then turned away, unable to face her plain indifference.

She'd packed the car herself the night before. She filled the trunk with clothes, a few of her favorite family pictures of her with their children, Pip and Leslie. She had agreed to take as little as possible from the household itself.

Her last morning here with them was to be a re-enactment of happiness.

Beth goes out to the woodpile to gather an armful of the damp wood. Startled, the geese take off from the pond. She stands in the driveway, and watches them fly over the fields out of sight, listening to their distant honks. "Want," she hears them cry, "Want, want, want, want, want." She hears the pop of gunfire and feels herself both accomplice and victim. The cinders in the driveway crunch underfoot as she walks back to the house.

Bob is standing in the middle of the living room, his arms hanging by his side. How long has he been waiting? She barely suppresses the annoyance in her voice to say, "Good morning."

"Good morning again." His tone reveals no pleasure in the irony of his response. "Do you want to build the fire yourself? or shall I do it?"

Given the choice, she doesn't mind relinquishing the task. He squats on the hearth, stacking the wood, crumpling newspapers underneath.

"We never did get around to repainting," she says. The paint over the fireplace is streaked from smoke and soot.

"We didn't get around to a lot of things," he says without turning to look at her. The flames lick, then catch into the wood. "I guess I didn't see things had gotten so bad. I thought there was plenty of time."

She hopes he won't say, "And there still can be." She perches on the arm of the sofa. The fire will hold though the wood pops and cracks like distant gunshots. She's eager to leave, to make her getaway, and her head fills with the nasal sound of her undefined desires, *want, want, want, want, want* like the squawk of the geese she'd just heard in their flight.

Backing down the long curving drive, Beth looks over her right shoulder to stay on the cinders, not wanting to leave tire marks in the wet lawn. She turns to wave one more time to Pip and Leslie. Leslie clings to Bob's legs as he stands on the porch holding Pip.

She could have predicted the phone call, "Leslie's teacher called. She hasn't been behaving in class. What do you want me to tell her?"

"Use your judgment. Be honest."

"I don't want to say too much. You might be back."

"I can call the school. I'm still her mother."

"Right. But you're not here. Pip walks around asking, 'Where did Mommy go?' about forty times a day. He's only two! What am I supposed to tell him? I know where you live, but I sure as hell don't know where you are."

"Neither do I."

"That's not funny."

"I'm not trying to be funny."

"OK. I know. I'm sorry."

"Me too."

"I just wish you'd come home. You belong here."

"Don't..."

"Bitsie. Bitsie Ellis." She's startled into nostalgia hearing her childhood name.

Twenty years ago when they were both teenagers this man had pulled her into her first demanding kiss. She feels herself blushing at the memory.

Ed is divorced, living in town. He thinks he remembers hearing she's married. Is she?

Before she answers, he reaches out and picks up the long end of her red scarf. The gesture startles her with its intimacy. "Is this the same one? Whenever I see a woman wearing a red scarf I think of you." He holds the scarf even after he finishes speaking.

The first time they kissed, they were standing on her porch, their breath puffs in the icy air. As he unwound the scarf the cold seared her neck, even before his lips touched her. All that winter as they huddled together in his car, he had a ritual of slowly unwinding her long red scarf. She'd hung on his neck as though she were drowning.

"No," she says, not clarifying whether she is answering his question about her marriage or her scarf, and she asks about his holidays. She doesn't want to talk about her separation. She could lie and tell him about the large stone house, the pond, her loving husband and darling children just as though she'd never left. If she tells the truth, he'll want to see her, to have dinner, to unwrap her again.

She makes the excuse of being late for an appointment, and promises to look him up in the phone book and call, to have lunch.

He adds, "Or maybe dinner?"

Something about her must have telegraphed the truth. She holds her body away from his in a stylish hug, then flees, clutching the red scarf.

It had snowed all night. She'd been warned that the children might be aloof on her return to punish her for leaving. When she pulls into the drive, Pip and Leslie look over at her from the other side of the yard where they're squatting. Then they go back to staring at something in the snow. Beth waves, then walks across to them. She looks down at their feet where she finds a few bloody globules, remnants of a night kill. Like garnets in light, they seemed to glow from within. "That's one of those things to look at, not touch, right, Mommy?" asks Leslie.

"Good girl, Les," she says. "Who wants a hug from Mommy?" She bends down to them. Neither one moves close.

"We're going sledding this afternoon," announces Leslie, "The hill by the lake. Daddy said we could."

"Down fast," adds Pip. Then he runs off to make loops around and around in the snow. "Go down fast." He flaps his arms like a bird.

Leslie takes off after him.

"I thought we'd have some time together first," Bob says. He stands without hat or coat at her side. "And they've been looking forward all winter to the sledding. I promised they could go with the Millers."

Her face was all reproach.

"It was the first good snow in a long time…."

"I didn't know my coming back would be so inconvenient."

"Come on," he lifts his gloveless hand as though to brush a strand of hair from her face, then lets his arm fall. "I got into the habit of making decisions by myself."

Beth stands at the window, pulling the heavy blue drape to one side. The trees are intricate skeletons against a pearl sky. The geese are gone, the pond frozen. She looks at the empty yard, the snow marked by the wild interlocking paths of Pip and Leslie. She wants the children home.

She lets the curtain fall and looks with the eye of a traveler returning to a familiar place. Bob has repainted the wall over the fireplace, and she resents the improvement. She notices a new pillow on the sofa. She buries her face in it, searching for another woman's perfume. Nothing.

She picks up the music box her in-laws had given Leslie and winds it to hear "Rock-a-bye Baby" as a carved wooden cradle jiggles up and down.

Beth had argued quietly with Bob. She didn't want the children to go sledding at the lake. Bob had insisted they'd be fine. She was afraid that the ice would be too thin, that they'd go down the hill and across the ice until they hit a spot where the ice would crack, and the sled would go crashing through and down, pulling the children into the cold, dark water.

She imagines Leslie's happy laughter, Pip's little voice crying, "Go down fast," and after the descent, the screams changing from delight to terror.

She takes her coat from the clothes peg in the hall, leaving her red scarf behind. It is only a few minutes drive to the hill and the lake. She turns up the collar of her coat. Bob stands in the doorway watching her.

"The kids are fine," he says before she has time to ask. "Fine."

"I'm going to the lake."

He moves toward her and puts his hand on her shoulder in a gesture of comfort, not restraint. "The kids are down the road at the Millers'. They'll be back in time for supper."

"Bob. . ."

"No, really. I just phoned there to make sure they'd be back by six-thirty."

"I still want to go to the lake." Her hand is on the doorknob.

"Company?" without waiting for an answer he follows her, pulling the door shut behind him. "I'll drive."

She hesitates for a moment before getting into the front seat beside him.

"Bitsy," he says, startling her with the nickname he rarely used. "Honestly, I am sorry. I wanted a little time with you first, and time for the kids to think of you as being at home without pressuring them."

She nods.

"You forgot your scarf. Do you want mine?" He reaches up to his plaid scarf.

"I'll be ok."

"All winter whenever I saw a woman wearing a red scarf I thought of you, but then, I often thought of you."

She stares straight ahead, thinking of Ed. They drive the rest of the way in silence.

"Where are all the children?" It's a foolish question. This late in the afternoon, all the children must have gone home.

"Do you want to get out and walk down?"

They stand at the top of the hill by the side of the road. The trammel of footprints and the tracks of the sleds cross and re-cross. She hunches down into her coat. When Bob puts his arm around her, she doesn't bother to pull away.

They'd brought first Leslie and then Leslie and Pip to the gravelly beach. In summer long grasses and blue pickerelweed edged much of the lake, and the bottom was muck although the popular beach area had been kept clear. Often she and Bob had stayed late, or had come back for a picnic supper at one of the tables. Sometimes at sunset the lake became a sheet of fire. The snow-covered grills stood like small grim white-hooded sentinels.

"Let's go," she says. They hold onto one another as they go down the hill and across the flat shore.

They follow the tracks of the sleds out over the snow-covered ice. "It'll hold us. Don't worry," Bob says.

They walk out to where their footsteps are the only marks on the snow.

"Look." She points to a spot about twenty feet ahead of them where the wind had blown the snow, clearing a patch of ice the width of her arms' span.

She pulls free of Bob to edge towards the spot where the ice changes from opaque to transparent.

She's as breathless as though she'd been running for a long time. She bends towards the void, holding herself in uncertain balance as she stares through the ice into the dark water at something red, floating suspended. What has the ice trapped? Her hands fly up to her bare neck.

Her throat is tight, and, lightheaded, she doesn't know if she has screamed. She's losing her balance. And then her husband is at her side, holding her steady.

"Beth, are you all right?"

Her voice is a low moan when she points, "Under the ice."

Bob peers down through the ice into the empty water. "What? I don't see anything."

"Bob, there was a scarf, a red scarf like mine. I was sure I saw it." But now, when she looks down she sees nothing but their blurred reflections.

"This ice looks pretty thick. It would have taken a long time to freeze this solid."

She nods in agreement. The ice is thick. "I must have been mistaken." Were their reflections an illusion too? "When I saw the scarf—thought I saw—it was almost as though I was the one under there."

She steps away from him. "And I knew I had to get out."

"I thought that's what you were doing when you left a few months ago."

"I wasn't really with you anyway."

"Beth, please..."

"I didn't understand then what was happening."

"And now you do?"

She looks up at him as he stands, a sturdy pillar against the sky.

"Maybe now I can begin," she said with a shudder.

"Are you cold?"

She has a quick vision of her red scarf on its peg in the hall. "Let's go back," she says, with an ambiguous but expansive gesture, "It's time to be going home."

COMFORT

When I got home from the Food Lion, Tom was striding across his lawn, a good ten feet ahead of Faydene, who had a green plastic leaf bag slung over her arm. He got to the small tree on the berm between their sidewalk and the street, nodded to me, and began plucking the leaves without waiting for Faydene to catch up. Faydene called out to me that Tom was "sick to death" of raking, and they were "going to get the last leaves before they fell."

She caught up to Tom and held open the bag. Without looking at me, she said, "I hear you've met our Beau."

I'd learned enough about living here so that I knew better than to ask how she'd heard. Tom dropped the handful of leaves he was clutching into the open bag. Was this how all of Carthage dealt with fall? I gestured to my lawn and promised I'd be getting to mine that afternoon. I had to. Tom's leaves would be all accounted for, and any new ones might as well have had a return address stamped on them

By the time I went back out, Faydene and Tom had gone. I set to work, raking and bagging the leaves. As I finished, a few more leaves drifted down, landing so far from one another that it made no sense to rake. Racing dusk, I walked the lawn and picked up each leaf, until my fists were full. I jammed the leaves into the bag and, when I'd got the last of them from the lawn, I stood for a while contemplating the few left on branches. I could use Tom's method. It wasn't better than raking, but it would be better than what I'd just done.

I went in and got a cardigan. I tied up the bag that was full, and held an empty bag, snapped it open, tore a hole near the top and slipped my arm through it. I began picking leaves from the first branch of dogwood and whispered, *"He loves me, he loves me not."*

All the colors dissolved in the evening air. Behind me my porch light glowed, and a full moon just cleared the trees. *He loves me, he loves me not.* How long would it take before Beau heard I was outside in the moonlight plucking leaves from my dogwood tree? I kept on task. *He loves me, he loves me not, he loves me.*

I knew there'd be leaves enough for me to get it right.

Beau acted like my own private welcome wagon. Not long after we met, he came by with a big sack of pecans from his tree. He'd washed and dried them and brought them with a nutcracker and picks. We spent the evening cracking enough for two pecan pies with plenty left over.

He brought along what he said was his family recipe, which uses both brown sugar and corn syrup. And he brought the brown sugar and a bottle of Karo. Two glass pie plates, too, brand new with the labels still on the bottom. And two bottles of chilled white wine, one with the label soaked off. He said it'd make a good rolling pin "in case I hadn't had a chance to unpack mine."

Even now, I have to give him this: Beau always wiped his feet at the door, and he never walked around my house in his stocking feet.

The day Beau took me to get mistletoe, whatever hope I had was as pretty as an antique Christmas ornament. I was treating it like that, too: something bright and shining, but hollow and fragile.

I thought we'd be going to the farm market on the highway, the one they keep open all winter, with the wood stove going in the middle and heaps of colorful citrus in the aisle bins, with winter squash, green and orange, down near the potatoes and waxed turnips.

We drove right by, didn't even slow down. I'd been quiet, thinking about how I would stay here for Christmas this year, try to make myself think of Carthage as home, hang lights, invite friends, invent my own traditions. Beau hadn't said much either. He talked in spells—some days he'd be like he was the day we'd met, saying things I would've had to work hard to think up, using more similes than a Surrealist poet on amphetamines. I hadn't trusted that wit at first; it seemed insincere, as though he had a writer somewhere feeding him lines through some invisible Bluetooth.

I whipped my head around when we passed the store. "We can stop on the way home, if you need something, Sugar," he said. "But first, we get the mistletoe."

"Where?" I asked, though I didn't care. I was happy just being with Beau.

"I have friends," he said, "with woods on their property."My failure to understand must have showed, because he went on, "Look," he said, "It grows all through here, those green things way up in those oaks? Mistletoe."

"You're kidding, right?"

"What did you think that was up there?"

"I hadn't noticed," I said. "It's so expensive, I can't believe it just grows—wild."

"Not just wild." He paused. "Mistletoe, Sugar, is a parasite."

"If it's way up on the trees, how do you get it down?"

He laughed again. "The way everybody does. How do you Yankees get it down?"

"We always went to the store to get it," I said.

"We shoot it."

It took awhile before I understood, and he seemed to enjoy my being puzzled.

After a visit with his friends, a couple whose flair for simile was as natural as moss on the north side of the trees, Beau and I headed out. The fallen oak leaves rustled as we walked. He'd taken his shotgun from its case at the car, and he carried it on his shoulder, whistling the theme from Peter and the Wolf.

This was the first time I'd been in woods without a path to follow. I was uneasy even with Beau, maybe because of him.

From time to time he'd stop and look up, then walk on again, until he stopped, pointed up and said, "Perfect."

I saw mistletoe in the upper branches of many trees. I didn't understand what was so special about this one. "You're going to shoot it?"

"Not from here," he said, "the angle's wrong. I'd have to shoot straight up. Too dangerous."

"Then why?" I asked.

"Tradition," he said. He took my chin in his hand and tilted my face up to kiss me. Once. "We don't need a great big red ribbon tied on the mistletoe for that, do we?"

"I guess we didn't," I said. It wasn't our first kiss, and I'd thought we didn't need the mistletoe, but I hadn't wanted to say as much myself.

Beau took me by the hand and led me over to a tree and told me to stay there. He walked off a bit, sighted up at the mistletoe and shot. It took a few tries. He looked and said what he'd got was female. Berries. "Toxic," he said.

He brought down three of these. We left one with his friends, and we took the others back to town. He gave me a whole one to divide and give to my friends. I knew he'd do the same, and I wondered how many kisses he'd be getting and from whom.

I tied the mistletoe bunches with red velvet ribbons. Tom and Faydene got one, of course, and I mailed some home with a note, but I left out the detail about my sending used goods. The kiss in the woods wasn't something they needed to know.

Even though he had plenty, I gave Beau a bunch I made up with red ribbon and silver bells. I wanted him to think of me when he got kissed under that mistletoe. And I'm pretty sure he was, at least the one time it mattered.

When I was just about feeling settled, Beau brought me branches of red camellias. I bent to smell the blossoms. Almost nothing. He laughed. "They are what they are," he said.

I put the branches in a cut glass vase. Beau stood leaning against the kitchen counter while I did the arranging. In the language of flowers, scarlet camellias meant "you're a flame in my heart". His hands jammed into his pockets, he intended nothing of the sort.

Within days the camellia blossoms fell whole from the branches. I floated the fallen flowers in a wide shallow bowl of water, and they sailed with nowhere to go, bumping up against the side of the bowl, darkening scarlet rafts adrift in currents too faint for me to see.

SCAR

L ong ago, before Ruth's cabinets held towers of canned soup and smaller towers of tuna and sardines, when her freezer was innocent of frozen diners, in other words, when she was so young that she could not imagine what her life could become, Ruth got naked with men. She took off her clothes as easily and lightly as now she slips into her pink cotton housecoat. Naked, she was content to lie in full light and never wondered if she was found pleasing. Then Ruth's body was untouched by gravity; her thighs, unmarked by veins, might have been bloodless. But it was neither vanity nor even self-assurance that kept insecurity at bay. She simply had no time to think about her body.

In bed, Ruth seemed entirely unselfish. She examined every square centimeter of her lovers, and followed her gaze with light brushes of fingers and lips. She seemed so tender and so passionate they never suspected it was not sex she wanted, that her touches and kisses were not born of affection, but were a ruse to hide her inspection of their bodies.

Though sex was not unwelcome, Ruth wanted more from the men she lay with, sliding into bed with them as soon as they piqued her curiosity. Only the youngest die unmarked, Ruth knew, and she divided scars into two sorts, accidental and surgical. All this happened before Lyndon Baines Johnson showed the country his new surgical scar, lifting the hospital gown for the photographer. No, then it was the accidental scars that produced stories of character. What Ruth wanted, truthfully, from her lovers were their stories.

These she drew from her lovers by offering little stories of her own. She showed them the scar on her palm. She told them how she had cut her hand pushing ice into a glass—how she had wanted to shape the world to suit her, and had a bloody lesson that the world would not accommodate her. She gave them the bandaged hand throbbing in the movie she'd gone to right after, *Psycho*, and the blood in the shower scene forever connected to her own profligate bleeding into the kitchen sink. She showed them the cinders embedded in her right knee, and told how she had slid into third base wearing a skirt because she hadn't gone home to change into play clothes after school. She gave them her mother's cigarette smoke rising into her eyes, already stinging with tears of angry humiliation, her mother's scolding all the while that she swabbed and bandaged Ruth's knee.

Having offered her own stories, she asked easily for theirs. Not all at once of course. She was the sultan to their Scheherazade. When no more stories were to be had, she abandoned the body and its owner with such kindness, with such delicacy, that each man would have sworn that he had left her.

And then she met Michael Walker, a wiry man who wanted to be called Mickey. Ruth thought Mickey looked as though he would have been at home in a taproom with a pack of Camels rolled into the sleeve of a white tee shirt. It was, however, deep in the underground library stacks of NYU that she met him. He was squatting, looking on the lower shelves for a book on T.S. Eliot, while she was looking for a book on Eliot, but on the higher shelves. Ruth, wearing a fashionable red mini-dress, nearly knocked Mickey over as she leaned above him to scan the titles. He didn't move to accommodate her, but looked up the length of her body through his rimless glasses, grinned and asked her if he could help her as she reached for a volume by Kenner that should have been in the reading room. "I can manage," she said in a tone he later told her was ungracious, but, in fact, she could not, and, reaching, lost her balance.

He held up his hand, and, without thinking she took it to steady herself and held it for a moment longer than necessary.

"If he had moved over," she thought "I could have done it. He stayed there on purpose." So the first time they touched was the first time she was suspicious of him. It was a moment of nonpareil intimacy.

In the next weeks the Village became their guiltless feast. They ate blonde brownies and drank coffee at Chock Full O'Nuts; they ate mushrooms and marrow on toast and drank beer at the English Pub on the Avenue of the Americas; they ate chocolate rum cake and drank espresso at the Peacock on West Fourth Street. They shopped at Balducci's and Babka and carried their food in paper bags down Ninth Street across town to the East Village where they cooked in his apartment near Avenue B. The big covered tub in the kitchen was both counter and table for their dinners. Some nights they filled the tub with warm water and took candlelit baths, the brick-walled room perfumed with sandalwood incense while they smoked and wondered what became of the rainbows in the bubbles. Once in the semi-darkness Ruth could not remember if it was winter or spring.

In the time before they were naked together, Ruth considered Mickey's penis. He was a lapsed Catholic, and though her net had been cast wide, it had been cast, until now, only among what she thought of as Her People. Her knowledge of foreskins was limited to marble statuary or paintings of cherubim, and she wondered if she would find a fleshy foreskin disgusting. But, after all, she saw that he had, indeed, been circumcised according to the fashion of the time and class, and thereafter she gave his penis, which was fairly unremarkable, no more thought than to the rest of his seemingly perfect body.

That apparent perfection puzzled Ruth. Many mornings and nights they lay together on the white cotton sheets of his bed, and her ministrations to him were minute and considered. But search as she did, his body was, as far as she could see, unmarked. She looked for a scar to find the truth it would reveal.

She was relentless in her searches, which invariably resulted in sex. For would any normal man expect a woman to undress him and touch and kiss him so thoroughly here and there and there again if she had not wanted to make love? And Ruth dared not articulate the object of her minute and increasingly frantic examinations.

They had told each other the stories one ordinarily tells new lovers, but because these stories were so ordinary, Ruth was left unsatisfied. She had become obsessed with his surface perfection, and she was convinced that someday she would find the scar that held his secret story. And because this scar was kept hidden, she believed the secret it concealed must be terrible and sordid.

She scolded herself for her suspicions, told herself that she had read too much literature based on the truth of original sin. But her suspicions persisted, unresolved. Nights of troubled sleep left dark circles under her eyes.

Ruth watched as Mickey revealed himself to be the perfect lover. He kissed her toes, and her fingertips, the inside of her wrist, the hollow of her throat. He smoothed the hair at her temples, traced her cheekbones with his tongue. He kissed her eyelids, left and right and left again. When Ruth's eyes fluttered open, she found herself looking into his dispassionate stare. He did not look away. She might have been gazing into a mirror, and at last she knew his terrible secret flaw. Neither of them had reason to see the other again.

LIAR

I was a bad girl. I was never allowed to clap the gray felt erasers. Instead, I watched the good kids go out onto the fire escape and return smiling. I envied their whitened hands and looked down at my own hateful palms. I made tight fists to make half-moon marks with my nails. I sat on my wooden chair at the too small table with the groove at the edge where I was supposed to put my pencil and a hole on the right side of the groove, an inkwell for ink we didn't have. The ghosts of other names haunted the surface of the desk, but I did not dare add mine

Sometimes I still dream of standing in a white cloud, embracing a heaven of chalk dust in afternoon sun.

One day a couple of us had to stay in at recess while the teacher, Miss F., went outside with the class. She was punishing us for breaking the rules. She told us to sit quiet at our desks until they all came back. Why did she expect we would do what she told us to do when she wasn't there to watch us?

I traced the ghost names with my pencil. I counted ceiling tiles and papers tacked on the bulletin board. I imagined constellations of invisible stars swirling in the blue sky.

One of the boys, the adenoidal boy, the boy with pink and crusty eyelids, went up to the front of the room to Miss Franklin's desk. *Hey, hey, hey, you'll get us in trouble.* We were never allowed to go to that desk, to touch her things (a row of books, a red glass apple, a green blotter with brown leather at the corners). *Hey, hey, hey.* His back was to us. What is he doing? *Hey, hey.*

I never told who peed under the teacher's desk. The puddle stayed on the floor all afternoon until we left to go home. Miss F. pretended she didn't see it, but I know she did. I could tell by the way she sat stiff at her desk while we did the times tables.

If I could talk to him now, I'd whisper his name. I'd say, "Don't worry, friend. Your secret's safe with me."

Hoops

We'd driven past miles of wild rose hedges on the way, each a tumble of pink bloom—I'd stopped exclaiming when I realized they weren't supposed to be anything special. We passed dozens of brown cedar shake cottages like the one in the photo on Jake's desk before he slowed to a stop. Four identical white SUV's sat along the road like a row of ducks. His became number five.

Jake's dad owned a dealership.

We left the luggage in the car and headed towards the voices and rhythmic thuds that came from the driveway where a basketball game was underway. Jake's twin brother, Todd, had the ball, and, when he saw Jake, called out, "Bro'!" and tossed the ball to him.

Jake bounced the ball, first with his right hand and then his left.

On the sideline with my retro purse still over my arm, I felt like an awkward shrimp.

Jake's two steps, dribbling, took him almost halfway to the basket. He pushed the ball up in a high curve to the rim where it bounced, rolled, and then, to a chorus of cheers, fell through the tattered net into Todd's hands.

Were they following rules? Todd looked around to pass the ball, and Jake stood, hands raised, not to receive, but to block Todd's throw. Who was on whose team?

Todd pivoted, facing me. Nobody stood between us.

I was still wearing sunglasses, but we might as well have locked gazes.

No one moved. Was Todd going to fake a pass to me and then make a break around Jake to the basket—or pass to someone near the basket?

"Marla!" Jake's sister, Jessie, who was standing across the drive called my name. What did she want? "Mar-la!" she said, this time making it a chant.

Once when she came to dinner, I found her in front of the open medicine chest. She said she was looking for aspirin.

"Second shelf," I said. "Next to the Tylenol."

"Does Jake still use a neti pot?" she'd asked, closing the mirrored door.

"Not really," I said. I offered her water even though she stood there empty handed.

"Mar-la!" Again, she made my name a chant. The others took it up, "Mar-la, Mar-la, Mar-la!"

I let my purse slip to the ground and hoped nobody would step on it.

I couldn't play worth shit, but I caught the ball. Not a scuff on it, and heavier than I remembered. The summer I was 12 my parents rented a cabin on a lake. It was as though some virus had eliminated every kid between the age of 8 and 17 but me. I read. I swam. I lay on the dock. And I spent hours doing free throws with an old basketball and a hoop with chipped orange paint and no net.

As I nudged through puberty's gate into adolescence, basketball brought back the misery of that summer; other than the required hours in gym class, which I tolerated, I had nothing to do with it.

"Mar-la!" They were clapping in rhythm now. All of them, Jake, too.

I wasn't that far from the basket. I bounced the ball once and held it at my waist. I stared at the hoop. I could smell the lake, the pines around the cabin, the sun-warmed dusty earth, the lemony Jean-Naté I doused myself with after every shower that summer. I bounced the ball again.

"Mar-la! Mar-la!"

I took a deep breath. If the body has memory for motion, my body's memory sent the ball up in a perfect arc. Instead I threw the ball high and hard to put it way up on the sloping garage roof. The ball rolled down, striking snow guards, zigzagging away from the basket. None of the others moved to pick up the ball when it landed or when it stopped near my feet.

It was mine.

As soon as the ball left my fingertips, I understood the connection between trajectory and destiny, where I was and how I got here, the purpose of hoops.

BEGGING OFF

Everybody thought Blake and Bunny Schwartz were the ideal couple: beautiful, graceful, elegant. They enjoyed the bounty of happy, uneventful childhoods, but as only children of only children, they grieved the absence of cousins, aunts, and uncles for their unborn. One year passed, and then another; they talked about trying, didn't try, didn't talk about not trying. Time lay before them like an endless silken quilt.

They kept their wedding cake in a silver and white tin provided by the caterer, tucked way back in the farthest corner of the freezer. Blake said that only the color kept it from looking like a casket. Bunny wrinkled her nose. He was right, and he'd spoiled it.

On their first anniversary both sets of parents took them out to celebrate, passing up dessert in the restaurant, thinking they'd share the defrosted wedding cake at home. Bunny passed around a Sara Lee butter streusel. Her mother and mother-in-law united against her: where was the wedding cake?

"We're saving it," Bunny said, passing the plate of Sara Lee.

"For what?" her mother asked, cutting a small slice, "the *Moshiach*?"

"The Messiah's not coming tonight," Blake's father said.

"Nothing keeps forever," her mother-in-law warned. Her raised eyebrow also suggested that cheesecake would have been a better choice. She took a sliver.

"So what?" Blake's father said. "What is, is."

"You're such a philosopher, Pop," Blake said, beaming as though he meant it.

"Like a sparrow, you're eating," Bunny's mother said to her *machetuneste*.

"Love keeps," Bunny's father said. Nobody said anything. He wondered if he'd spoken aloud.

"For grandchildren you're waiting, maybe?" Bunny's mother said.

"For grandchildren," Bunny's mother-in-law said. "Who doesn't want a little *naches*?"

"*Sha,* still!" Bunny's father said. "They're not children!"

"They're our children," Bunny's mother-in-law said, glaring.

"Well, excuse me!" Bunny's father said. He hoped Blake didn't take after his mother.

"It's late," Blake's father said, making a show of looking at his watch, "And tomorrow's another day."

"We should leave the love birds to themselves," Bunny's mother said.

"These lovebirds are going home," her father said, hauling himself up from the easy chair, his favorite place to sit in their living room.

"Clean your engagement ring, *Bubbeleh*," Bunny's mother said, stopping a moment at the door, "Such a nice stone, let the light come through. It should sparkle like your eyes." She kissed her on the cheek. She'd talk about the grandchildren when they were alone.

"It got cold while we were inside," Blake's father said as he stood on the porch. "They didn't say...," His voice trailed off, and he shook his head, amazed at another betrayal.

Past the traditional first anniversary, Blake and Bunny waited for the right special romantic occasion to open the tin. Looking back, they agreed it had been their first significant fight, but neither could remember who had wanted to open the silver casket and who had been opposed—only the shrieking that proved it was the wrong time.

FLAMINGOS

Icy snow ticked against the windowpanes, and Jamie was sorry that she hadn't washed them in October before Mike moved in. Snow heaped up on the sills and blew in drifts over the sidewalk and on the small patch of lawn. Snow swirled around the six plastic flamingos that shimmied in the wind.

She had carried them home, a yard-sale treasure. "Six for five dollars! I've always wanted these."

"You wanted those...flamingos?"

"Oh yes," she said, thinking she wouldn't have bought them, would she, if she hadn't wanted them?

Everyone she'd passed had smiled at the flamingos, at her, and she'd smiled back as though they were sharing an old favorite joke. Jamie looked around for a place to put them down.

"They're dirty," Mike said, keeping his distance.

When had he become so fastidious? "Just the part that goes in the ground. They were pulling them up just as I arrived."

"And?"

"I said I'd take them all," she said.

"So they didn't even offer?" He frowned.

"I told them I'd be putting them in the yard right away anyhow." She shifted the weight of the birds. They were heavier than she'd expected they'd be. They were too dirty to put on the rug or table. Why hadn't she thought of leaving them on the porch instead of bringing them in to show him? "We will be, won't we?" she asked.

"You can if you want to," he said. "You might as well put them in the way you like." He shrugged his shoulders.

He might as well have said, "It's nothing to do with me."

"I guess there's more to it than I thought," she said. "Maybe for now I'll put them on the kitchen floor."

Mike stood between her and the kitchen, and he didn't move. She could walk around him.

"I guess they'll be in the way?" she said.

Mike smiled. She'd wanted to see that smile since she'd arrived with the flamingos.

"Won't they be in the way when I mow the lawn?"

She took care not to shrug her shoulders as he had done. "You won't have to mow again for months, and I can leave plenty of room. I'll put them on the porch for now."

Other people manage, she thought. Did the family she'd bought them from have a lawn or white stones out front? Stones. But some people have lawns and geese and gnomes and flamingos. "Or you can move them if you have to."

Mike stood next to her at the window watching the snow. He hadn't said anything for a long time, and she had been quiet, too. "They look ridiculous out there in the snow."

"That's the point. They're supposed to look ridiculous."

A gust of wind blew loose snow from the porch roof down into the yard, showering the flamingos.

"The poor things are cold," she said and waited for him to tell her she was wrong.

BIBLIOPHILE

Erin spent a long time trying to remember the title.
She tried *Way to Go* and *Suicide for the Masses*.

Then Christie told her the title, *Final Exit*.

Erin told herself it was only academic. After all, she had Emily Post.

She had never used that. Well, maybe just once.

She bought it. Used it. Once.

FOUR THINGS I FOUND

Paper poppy. At the back of his desk. He wore it home in his lapel. He told me about his favorite uncle who'd been in the war. He curled the stem around a yellow Ticonderoga pencil (number 2), then slipped the flower off the pencil and handed it to me to wear as a pinky ring. I took it off and put it on the kitchen counter while I prepared dinner. When it got wet, the flower left a red stain.

Coffee mug. In the dishwasher. Handmade pottery, blue and white glaze. We had purchased two in a shop in Cape May during our first weekend together. Identical. When one broke in the dishwasher, he said it was mine that broke. Who loaded the pot on top of the china? The cast-iron enameled pot?

Wallet. On his bureau. The leather was stretched and worn smooth, thin. An old driver's license. A photo of me smiling. He stopped carrying it, he told me, because one of his friends was mugged and lost all his family photos. He never cut up old credit cards. He kept them in this wallet with a few receipts, phone numbers in pen and pencil on the back of the receipts. I could phone them all, one after the other.

Empty bottle of Ambien. Top shelf of the medicine cabinet. No refills. "What's this?" I asked when I found the pharmacist's bag in the trash. I should have asked to see the bottle and counted the pills. He'd pour himself a drink every night when he got home and another at dinner. Skye vodka from the freezer. Red jug wine kept in the fridge. He said it was good for the heart.

HIDING:
A STORY WITH A HAPPY ENDING

She liked to walk behind him. She wondered at his wide shoulders and the way his tee shirts fell to his waist and hung in loose waves of fabric over his faded jeans. She liked to watch him walk bare foot, padding into the kitchen, and she followed him there using any old excuse. As long as he kept walking and didn't turn around, as long as he didn't see her face as she looked at him, he'd never know. She would be safe.

Because this is a story with a happy ending it goes like this: And then one day he turned around without warning. She knew her face gave her away. But he only said something about milk and nothing about her face. She remained safe. That is the happy ending, isn't it?

SURFACE WOUNDS

When Dan's ex-wife sold their house and moved to an apartment in Florida with their four kids, she left him with McIntyre, their longhair cat. The night before she drove straight down I95, Dan took custody of the cat, a carrier, two stainless bowls, a brush, and half a bag of kitty litter. I am allergic to cats.

Deedee, his youngest, carried McIntyre into Dan's apartment herself. She cradled him, cooing baby talk while Dan went out to her mom's car for the cat paraphernalia. "Dad says you're allergic," she said without looking at me. She buried her face in McIntyre's fur.

Allergies aren't character flaws, but you'd never know that from her tone. "I wish I weren't," I said.

Even though I didn't want McIntyre here, I was sad for her and Dan.

Dan came in, and Deedee set McIntyre down on the green plush sofa. McIntyre dashed into the bedroom.

"I didn't remember that he had so much stuff," Dan said, dropping most of it on the sofa, but setting the carrier on the floor.

"Mom didn't send the litter box. She said you could manage that."

Dan winced. We'd bought a litter box and food when we knew McIntyre was going to be moving in.

They wrapped their arms around one another. I didn't want to watch them say good-bye. I put my hand on Deedee's shoulder, "Your dad will look after McIntyre. He'll miss you." I left it ambiguous, murmured goodbye, and followed McIntyre into the bedroom.

I got on my hands and knees to see if I could spot him under the bed.

"He'll come out when he's ready," Dan said. I hadn't heard Deedee leaving.

"Before bedtime, I hope."

"He likes to sleep on the bed," Dan said.

"So do I," I said, trying not to sound cranky. "Do you think we can keep the bedroom cat-free?" I cleared my throat and coughed.

"I didn't have a choice," he said.

We all have choices. I got up and washed my hair. When I came out of the bathroom the bedroom door was closed. I knocked.

"I'm in the living room," Dan said. He sat on the sofa, with McIntyre on his lap. He didn't look up when I came in.

I raised my right eyebrow and said, "I see."

"What did you want me to do?" he asked. McIntyre jumped off his lap, rubbed once against my wet legs, and headed off to his food dish.

What I wanted was unreasonable, so I didn't tell him.

"We can keep the bedroom door closed," he said. "And I'll vacuum before we go to bed."

I smiled, but it was forced. How often would he have to vacuum so I wouldn't feel as though I had a hairball in my throat and a cat sleeping in my chest?

We'd just finished dinner when McIntyre came into the room. He stank. Dan picked him up and held him at arm's length. "Diarrhea again," he said as he carried him to the kitchen sink, which was, mercifully, empty of dishes.

"I need your help," he said.

McIntyre wriggled as Dan lowered him towards the sink.

"What do you want me to do?"

"If we don't clean him off, he'll get it on everything," Dan said.

I knew what "it" was. Dan was used to it. He'd done this before. And he hadn't warned me. No wonder Lana didn't want him with her.

I grabbed the dish drainer and lifted it.

"I told you I needed your help," Dan snapped. "Put that back."

I set the drainer on the counter across the kitchen.

"I need help with McIntyre, not with housekeeping."

McIntyre yowled. I know how you feel, buddy, I thought.

"Hold him," Dan said. "Hold him steady."

Dan stepped back without letting go. McIntyre's paws were in the air. He was clawing, wild.

Dan lowered McIntyre further into the sink. McIntyre's claws scrabbled against the metal.

I reached towards his body. His forelegs flew up and grabbed at my arm. A claw hooked into my arm and I pulled back, leaving a long deep scratch.

"I told you—careful," Dan said.

I looked at my bleeding arm.

"Come on," Dan said, "this isn't going to get easier."

I can believe that, I thought. "You have to move back so I can reach him. My arms aren't as long as yours."

Dan stepped back without letting go. "Now," he said.

"How often does this happen?" I wasn't sure what answer to expect.

"I said grab him!"

"I'm trying," I answered. I tried to hold McIntyre's body, without being in reach of his claws.

McIntyre's crying sounds like a baby. He twisted first one way and then another, paws out, but I got both hands on him.

As long as Dan held him, too, it was all right.

"Hold him. He's not going to like this!" Dan reached for the sink's hose and let go of McIntyre.

The cold water poured over my hands onto McIntyre's torso. He yowled and twisted, paws clawing the air, frantic. But I held on and tried to keep him from scratching me again.

Dan put soap on his hand, then squirted and sudsed McIntyre's rear. Before Dan could rinse him, McIntyre twisted free, gouged my arm again, and vaulted up and out of the sink, across the cleared drain board to freedom.

"Look what you've done now!" Dan screamed. "I can't count on you at all!"

Dan's face reddened. "We've got to get him back up here and rinsed off."

"Or?" I said.

I heard McIntyre scratching in the kitty-litter. "Or the whole thing will have been for nothing," Dan said. "Useless," he hissed, looking straight at me.

I rinsed and washed my scratched arm in the sink. It stung, but the scratches would heal without a trace.

Sugar Ants

No matter how many times Carol Lee scrubbed, she looked for the stain whenever she sat at the kitchen table. The cup she hurled had nicked the wall and splattered coffee in a dark starburst with streamers running down into the crack between the wall and baseboard. Three teaspoons of sugar in the coffee invited a persistent infestation of sugar ants.

She hated the heavy diner-style cup, and wasn't sorry to smash it. She hadn't aimed at her husband. She'd intended the cup to whizz by Frank's head, just to get him to look up from his laptop, to talk to her instead of click click clicking, meal after meal.

She imagined the miniscule feet of the sugar ants inaudible on the tile floor, invisible on the fancy granite counter.

The cup, sailing within inches of his ear, failed to get Frank's attention, but he looked up at the sharp sounds of the cup hitting the wall, the china shattering on the floor, and Carol Lee's wordless wail of outrage.

"Something wrong?" His tone was empty of irony.

She was furious with him but more so at herself for reverting to what she thought of as "trash." She was also a bit short of breath. The cup had come closer to hitting him than she'd expected, but he had no way of knowing that.

"Wrong? Do I throw cups at the wall every morning?" At the wall. That ought to make her intentions clear.

Her mother taught her to hate sugar ants when they appeared on the speckled green linoleum tiles, the white Formica counter, the porcelain sink board. They made her mother crazy. Vinegar. Hot water. Ammonia. They always came back. Now they were here.

Before she pushed her chair away from the table, she hadn't decided whether she'd walk right out of the kitchen or clean up. She'd done enough damage. She bent to get the largest shards and dropped them in the trash. She grabbed five or six paper towels. Squatting, she wiped the coffee from the floor and used the same paper towel to pick up the smaller pieces within a three-foot radius. She'd wet-mop the sticky floor later.

"Need help with that?"

Good Lord above, while she was down there cleaning up the slivers of china, Frank was clicking away on those computer keys.

"What will it take, Frank?" She spoke from a crouching position, balanced on the fingertips of her free hand. Would he think she's cowering, or ready to spring? White shards were under Frank's chair, too. She'd get those later.

"I am not tactful like you," she said, pronouncing each syllable as though she were reading from a formal script. She'd screamed these words at him many times in her imagination. Never before, however, had she even thought of hurling something at, that is, past him.

"You can be," he said. "You're the soul of tact when you think it counts."

Throwing cups, well, that was nothing to do with tact. That was a whole other category of rhetoric, but he would never say so. Instead he accused her of undervaluing him. Carol Lee's face burned. Without looking in a mirror, she knew each cheek had a red spot like a clown's. It happened whenever she was humiliated.

How small would she have to be so she could hear them? *Click click click.* They marched from behind the baseboard and the dried sweet coffee that would be there forever.

That was what this was about. Undervaluing. "Thank you," she said.

She wouldn't say she was sorry until she meant it.

"I won't be home for dinner tonight," she said, surprising herself with her declaration. Where would she go?

He raised an eyebrow, then clicked at the computer. "I don't see anything here."

"Not everything's on the computer," she said. She stood over him. She held the wadded-up paper towel with the slivers of the smashed cup. The computer was open, vulnerable. Screen. Keyboard.

He looked at her straight on, his face as blank as a dark screen, and clicked the computer closed. He'd slide it into its case and take it with him when he left. "I'll fend for myself, then."

She tossed the damp paper into the garbage. What was the rule for broken china? How small did the piece have to be before it disqualified itself from the recycling bin?

She'd start on the wall when he left. She couldn't let the stain set in. She'd have to do the whole wall. You can't clean just a small spot. Ever. She'd learned that early on in their marriage, getting a bit of jam off the wall. That had been an accident; Frank had tossed a jammy napkin into the trash and missed. A wall isn't a backboard.

Had she been tactful then? She couldn't remember what she'd said, only the hours of scrubbing.

"I won't be late," she said, "not too late." She could always say she had a change of plans and be home, fix dinner, hope he'd be there.

He'd be too tactful to quiz her. Or too indifferent. He wore his good manners like a mask.

She clenched her teeth. She'd have to remember not to go barefoot. No matter how she tried to clean up, weeks after an accident some sliver of glass showed up underfoot. She had cuts to prove it. She'd been raised to believe that only a slattern goes barefoot in the house. She went barefoot anyway.

Sweet coffee behind the baseboard? She'd set out a permanent buffet. Frank, she thought, would ignore sugar ants even in his own home, like it's bad manners to attend to vermin. One day it would get so he'd have to pay them some mind; by then the damage would be irremediable.

More than one cup had shattered on this floor. Anything they dropped broke. Tile floors were unforgiving too.

MIRIAM N. KOTZIN is Professor of English at Drexel University where she teaches creative writing and literature. She was the founding director of the Certificate Program in Writing and Publishing. *Country Music* joins her collection of flash fiction, *Just Desserts* (Star Cloud Press 2010), a novel, *The Real Deal* (Brick House Press 2012), and five collections of poetry *Debris Field* (David Robert Books 2017), *The Body's Bride* (David Robert Books 2013), *Taking Stock* (Star Cloud Press 2010), *Weights & Measures* (Star Cloud Press 2009), and *Reclaiming the Dead* (New American Press 2008),. Her poetry received six nominations for a Pushcart Prize. Her work has been published widely in such places as *Shenandoah, Boulevard, Eclectica, The Tower Journal,* and *Valparaiso Poetry Review.* She is founding editor of *Per Contra* and has been a contributing editor of *Boulevard* since its inception.

www.ingramcontent.com/pod-product-compliance
Lightning Source LLC
Chambersburg PA
CBHW020657260626
47157CB00008B/3064